One Last Night To Love

By: H. Matt Synnot

Table of Contents

Chapter 1

The Phone Call

Peter Lowry had just walked in the door of his home as heard the phone ringing. This always seemed to happen and he hated it.

Peter was thirty five years old and had just finished a long day of work at the utility company where he had to work after a storm restoring power. Although by now he was the actual head of the entire maintenance division in emergencies like this it was all hands on deck in the field and it actually felt good from time to time to be out with the guys. He sighed as he briskly walked over to the phone and picked it up.

A woman's voice was on the other end of the phone. "Is this Peter. Lowry?"

He didn't have a chance to glance at the caller ID so he answered "Yes it is" followed by the dumb question "Who is calling?"

"This is Alex Foreman from the state Department of

Corrections."

Peter sighed. This could only be about one thing. "Yes what do you want?"

"Your wife Alicia has been approved for a brief compassionate leave from her sentence to attend her mother's funeral in two days and she has requested permission to stay with you the night before the funeral so she can attend because of the distance."

Peter closed his eyes. It was Alicia again intruding into his life. It had been a living hell with the notoriety and he thought he was done with her and now this brought everything out again. He couldn't deal with it. "She's not my wife anymore, we're divorced."

There was a momentarily silence on the other end. "I see. Would you still be willing to give your permission? We do need someone she can stay with."

"I'd prefer she stay with someone else, Mrs. Foreman."

"She says she had only had her mother if I recall. Her father died many years ago and she has no siblings."

"So what if I don't agree?"

More silence. "Uh that makes it awkward. We'd have to deny the leave. You know how much trouble it will cause us to cancel it at this point. Would you be willing to let her come? It's just one night."

3

Peter remembered Alicia's mother and she was a decent loving woman and deserved having her daughter at the funeral. "How would that work? Do you folks understand what she tried to do? What if she runs off?"

"Believe me she'll have an ankle bracelet and it will be VERY closely monitored. If you want we can have an officer posted right outside your home. Of course, it's up to you Mr. Lowry."

"Who will know about this?"

"We don't publicly announce compassionate leave so nobody will. She's been a model inmate and we're afraid if she doesn't get the chance t do this she'll become disruptive."

"One night, that's all?"

"Yes Mr. Lowry, one night." There was a pause. "We can have our staff drop her off in an unmarked car and then we'll collect her in the morning to attend the funeral and then she'll be transported right back to the facility."

"It's against my better judgment, but fine if it'll help your situation I'll do it, but while she's here I don't want to deal much with her, and yes I do want that officer."

Alex then confirmed his address and said that they should be there with Alicia around six thirty pm two days from then and then they exchanged some pleasantries before Peter hung up.

Chapter 2

Ghosts of the Past

Peter went to the frig and pulled out a beer and sat on the couch and begin to sip and as he closed his eyes, the memories flooded back into his mind. He could still envision Alicia the first day he met her. She had bright red hair and the first thing about her that attracted his attention was her laugh. He looked over and just at that moment she looked back at him and he could already see the green sparkling eyes even from about fifteen feet away. She was wearing a bright red strapped dress that ended just above the knees that showed off her shapely and well defined legs. The dress was cut low enough that it showed off a bodice of beautifully round yet just the right sized breasts.

He couldn't seem to take his eyes off of her, even though he was dressed quite casually in jeans and a tight muscle shirt. Yes he still dressed like that when he was twenty five, and if he had to guess her age, he'd guess that she was in her early twenties.

As much as he wanted to approach her, he ignored his impulses and instead went over to the pool table and before long was able to play. He was pretty good at it then and had just won his fourth straight game when he felt a presence in back of him. In a feminine voice that sounded almost musical he heard the words: "Looks like you're the best player in here, aren't you?"

Peter turned around and was face to face with the girl in red and grinned. "Well let's say I'm pretty good."

She grinned. "I can always spot a winner. My name's Alicia. Alicia Townsend."

"Peter Lowry. Never saw you here before."

"Just moved here from about thirty miles away to live with my Mum."

"Oh is she ill?" She gently shook her head, but then he thought he saw a tear in her eye. "Did I say something wrong?"

"No, just some sad things happened."

"So it's just you and your Mom then?"

"No there are my two boys."

"Really? You don't look that old, Alicia."

She beamed. "Yeah I'm twenty three and had them young." Then she grinned. "Do I really look that young, Peter?"

"You sure do. What happened to their Dad?"

He saw some more tears form. ""He died last year."

"I'm so sorry, Alicia. What happened?"

"It was a terrible accident. I'd rather not talk about it OK? Can we just have some fun tonight?"

"How old are the boys?"

"The oldest is four and the youngest is two. It's so hard but at least Mum can help out sometimes so I can just get out. I don't know where we'd be if it hadn't been for Jake's insurance."

"I'm glad he was that thoughtful Alicia. Still must be rough."

Her eyes still glistened from the tears but then she smiled. "But there's tonight and all the other nights and I know he'd want me and the boys to be happy. Can we not talk about sad things anymore?"

He smiled and much to the relief of the other contestants gave up the table and Peter and Alicia walked over to a small table in the corner after they each got a beer. "So what are you going to do while you're here now?"

"Luckily there's enough money I don't need to work and I can just focus on Mikey and Alan."

"Those your boys?"

"Yup. Mikey the hellion two year old and Alan's the oldest always so serious. So what do you do?"

He told her about working for the utility and was just starting out but was hoping to move up in the company. "Do you look down on me because I work with my hands?"

She smiled and took one of Peter's hands in hers. "They look like nice strong hands, Peter." As he felt her touch he felt a shiver go through his body.

"So when did you move here?"

"Oh last week. It just got to be too much and the boys weren't seeing much of their Grandma. They were spending a lot of their time with Jake's parents instead and they were stifling me."

"Jake was your late husband?"

"Yeah, like I said I wish we could talk about something else."

So they started talking about movies and music and he couldn't believe how much in common they had. When he talked about an upcoming movie that hadn't been released yet, Alicia blurted out: "So why don't we go watch it together?"

Peter had cocked my head. "Are you asking me out Alicia?"

I heard that laugh again. "Sure, Why should I have to wait for you to do it because I can tell you wanted to didn't you?" As she said that she took his hand in hers.

I blushed. "Yeah I guess I did."

"Then it's settled. Are you free on Wednesday?"

"Well after work I am. I get out at 5:30."

She opened her purse, took out a pen and paper and wrote down an address. "Here's my address, I'll expect you at 6:30 then."

"What if the movie is later."

Her eyes sparkled in the light. "Well then we can just have a drink first can't we?" As she said it she squeezed his hand.

"Or maybe after." Peter said as he squeezed back and

already was feeling a stirring in his groin.

They had another beer together and were talking and laughing and she was so easy to talk to and funny and yet seemed so smart and honest. It seemed much too soon when Alicia said: "Oh Peter, I do need to get back and help Mum put the boys to bed. I'm really looking forward to Wednesday."

Peter remembered smiling and responding: "So am I."

She slightly turned her head. "You know something tells me that we're going to get to know each other better, much better before this is all done." As Alicia said that she lightly touched him again and the stirring got even stronger.

"I think I'd like that Alicia." As she walked away, Peter's nostrils were filled with a light scent that he knew came from her and as she left the bar, he already couldn't wait for the time when he'd see her again.

Peter opened his eyes and looked around the room and saw the beer in his hand and he took another deep gulp. It had seemed so wonderful at the time and for years afterward but now he was wishing that night had never happened.

Chapter 3

Harsh Reality and Sweet Memories

Alicia Lowry was laying on her cot staring at the ceiling. The shadows formed by the light against the barred window in the door made its familiar pattern on the floor of her cell.

She could hear Kristen, her cellmate soft breathing in the bunk across the cell as she slept. Looking around she knew everything was all too familiar to her now. She had gazed upon the same scene for almost seven years now, and even Kristen was very familiar since they had been cell mates for all that time. In fact she realized that she had actually been with Kristen more than twice as long already as she had been able to be with Peter.

Alicia had a totally different set of memories to fill h thoughts than Peter did. The most dominating one was the words of the judge that seemed to replay in her mind every night. "Alicia Lowry, you stand before me having been duly convicted of first degree murder and therefore the Court sentences you to a term of life imprisonment without the possibility of parole." She could still recall the totally numb feeling she had as she heard her sentence, even though her lawyer had told her that is what the law required. Then the judge continued: "Mrs. Lowry, I suggest you use the years you have ahead of you to reflect upon how your actions impacted so many others, and although nothing can bring

Jake Townsend back to life, perhaps as you live the rest of your life in the custody of the Department of Corrections you'll be able to find a way to atone for your actions."

As those words flooded back into her mind, she looked down at the bright orange top and pants that she wore everyday as her uniform that reminded her every day that the days when she could wear beautiful and stylish clothes were gone forever now. She could still visualize the last time she could express herself that way with the outfit she wore to her sentencing. She had picked it out specially for that day because she knew after that fateful day she would never wear something she chose for herself again. It was a navy blue skirt with a matching jacket and the jacket had white trim on it and underneath was a bright white blouse. The skirt was nice and tight because on that one day she wanted desperately to show off her body to the media that was all over the story, but when she thought of that day she felt some tears once again because one thing conspicuous was that although Mum was there, neither Peter nor Alan or Mikey were there, although Jake's parents and his sister were at the hearing and had spoken bitterly and angrily about Alicia before the actual sentencing.

Peter had already filed for divorce before the hearing and when Jake's parents spoke at the sentencing, they spoke about their loss and also how difficult it was to tell their grandchildren who were then eight and six years old that their Mom had murdered their Dad and when Mrs. Townsend spoke she made it clear that she desired that the Department of Corrections ensure that there would be no communication between the children and Alicia. True to their word, Alicia never received anything from them, not a phone call, or card or even an acknowledgment that she even existed in their minds even after seven years.

On the day of the sentencing though Alicia was determined not to show weakness, nor publicly shed tears. She knew no matter what she did or say, nothing would change so why bother even though she knew that the media portrayed her as cold and heartless. The other inmates in the jail told her that if she was ever to survive as a pretty young woman in prison, nobody must ever see any weakness. From the moment she stepped off the van that took her to the prison as a convict she had followed that advice, and never cried, and always made sure that everyone there saw that hard, calculating edge to her.

Alicia closed her eyes, and lazily ran her hands over her body. She was thirty four now but her hands could still feel a pair of breasts that still had their firm bouncy texture and as those hands roamed down her flat stomach and even lovingly caressed her muscular thighs she knew that her body had remained youthful even after seven years being locked up. Yes it was still a body that was young enough to still be desirable, but as she looked in the mirror every day, she could almost see a new line or slight wrinkle in her face, and would when having the time look carefully to see if there were any beginnings of gray in her hair and as she felt her body right now and cherished it, she also knew there would come that time when age and the prison conditions would take their inevitable toll so that the firmness wouldn't be there, and her once desirable breasts would sag, the wrinkles on her face would become more pronounced and her hair transform from it's current bright red to gray just like her Mum's did..

Yes she had killed Jake, she thought. He had become controlling and never wanted her to have any fun anymore. She hadn't planned for it to happen when it did but there was that insurance money as consolation. Five hundred thousand dollars meant freedom, and she had hoped that she would be allowed to move on and do things she could only have dreamed of doing before when Jake's oppressive presence was around.

It all had started with a whimsical thought. Getting Jake out of her life meant things would be so different. At first she shook off the idea of it meaning actually killing him but the fantasy kept nagging at her and so she began to plot, saying to herself it was just a game. Ideas became strategy and strategy became plans. There would be an accident, yes an accident.

She had it all worked out and she was shaking when she realized that she might actually do it. I'd always make it so I could back out if I wanted she thought, but then there was the idea of a dry run when he didn't suspect it, and it would so damned easy to do just that.

Yeah, she tried a dry run but it didn't end up that way. She was scared for a moment, but managed to keep her cool and it went like a charm. A few questions from the police, but they bit on the story, the coroner called it an accident and a few months later the insurance money was in her account. She was free, finally free of that domineering husband and had all that money but suddenly realized she had the boys on her own, though everyone around hr was so sympathetic.

Jake's parents were understanding as well, but Alicia was also one who now wanted to go out and start living again. After all she was only twenty four and she shouldn't have to spend the rest of her life in mourning.

Now she understood how Jake had become as controlling as he had been. It was from those damned parents of hers, especially that shrewish mother of his. They were becoming stifling and almost as bad as he had been and she didn't even have the benefits of being married. Then after six months, Jake's mother started asking Alicia questions about Jake's accident. At first the questions were occasional but as time went on they became a little more persistent.

She had to get away from them with their dominance and

especially the questions and realized that Mum offered the perfect chance to do so. Mum had a nice comfortable home and could watch the boys a couple of nights a week and not ask anymore damned awkward questions. Finally a year after Jake's death, she finally announced the move, to the middle of the state and away she went.

Then there was the time she went out to this local bar, and she happened to look over and see this real hot looking guy playing pool. Even now, as she recalled it her tongue hungrily licked her lips as she remembered standing there and checking him out, and wondering what was inside those tight sexy jeans he wore, and that shirt stretched so taut over what she imagined was a compact muscular set of pecs and a flat stomach. He had a effortless fluid way of walking and the way he maneuvered his way around that pool table like he owned it made her know she just had to meet him. A few questions to the bartender helped her discover he was a regular and came in certain nights, and next time she'd be noticed.

So next time she wore that $400 flowing bright red dress and when she saw he was there made sure she was in the line of sight. Finally she noticed him looking over at her and she looked back and gave him a long enough look so that he must have know that she noticed him.

Now she was back in the present and moaned

"Mmmmmmmm, Peter." As she did so, she began to finger that special place and began to move her fingers back and forth and around. Oh such a waste, she thought. In that moment, in a different world, he'd be making passionate love to her right now. Her body always had an insatiable appetite for it and as her hands moved more rapidly, the tension increased inside her and as her excitement grew she let out a soft moan, but had learned over seven years to stifle them and hold the pleasure inside her as it grew until she knew there would be one loud groan, but Kristen was used to it by now because Alicia would occasionally hear the same from Kristen and just lay there and feign sleep and just know exactly what was going on but say nothing about it the following morning, although usually when they felt the need they would find comfort in each other.

Kristen was also in for life, but was lucky to have a potential release date in another nineteen years. She was thirty six and had been here for eleven years already, and Alicia would think of what it must be like for her to know that if she was fortunate to get paroled the first time, which very few did, she would be fifty five and have spent almost all her twenties and then her thirties and even forties in this awful place. Alicia had been able to enjoy almost all her twenties as a free woman, yet on the day Kristen finally walked out of here, Alicia knew she would still be here until the day she died. Which was worse, she wondered, to have had those priceless youthful days out and around knowing after them there was just this, or was it preferred to have lost those days and be able to live those mature years in freedom? She shook her head to clear those kind of musings because it just reminded her of the nightmare her life had become.

Yes she had to admit that sometimes the emptiness and loneliness became too much for them and they would often find comfort in each other. The first time it happened after two months in the same cell, when Kristen seemed to sense that the isolation and loneliness that Alicia was feeling.

It was during a night like this and Alicia was thinking of Peter and restlessly stirring on her bunk and contemplating having her hands wander over her body. Suddenly she felt a presence above her and saw Kristen looking down at her. At that time, Alicia was twenty seven and Kristen slightly older at twenty nine. Kristen's long blond hair flowed past her shoulders and her identical uniform concealed a well maintained body that was also still young and alluring, although her expression was almost always hard and lacking of any emotion. Since they were cellmates, Alicia couldn't help but notice her still hourglass figure and round, compact and muscular buttocks and larger, but perfectly formed breasts and that her well toned legs came together with a small blond patch of hair that barely hid her vagina. She had light blue eyes and a perfect set of white teeth and a button nose that was centered on her high cheek bones with lips that had the look of sensuality, especially s now when Kristen was occasionally licking them. As Alicia looked up at her Kristen sat down on the bed. "From what I see it looks like you could use some company."

Alicia lied even as she was able to admire,one woman to another, the way she looked. "I'll be alright, Kristen."

Suddenly, Kristen's hard expression seemed to soften. "If you were alright you wouldn't be so restless. I've been in this place four years and I know it sometimes feels like the walls are closing in on you." As she said that, her hand very tentatively brushed against Alicia's face.

Alicia felt a momentary shiver. "I know what you want but I'm not like that, Kristen"

Her expression hardened again. "It's about time you start facing reality, princess. You're going to be in here for a long, long time and it can either be a very lonely place or you can choose to make it a little more bearable."

"I don't know."

Kristen's hand moved lightly down Alicia's body,which slightly shivered. "I won't do anything, you don't want princess, but I can sense what you need, don't I? When was the last time anyone touched you?"

Alicia closed her eyes and then recalled the night before

her arrest. "Too long."

Kristen casually lifted up Alicia's top and ran her fingers lightly across Alicia's stomach and said "Then maybe it's time." Then she placed the fingers of her other hand on Alicia's head and started running them through Alicia's hair. "Anyone ever tell you that your hair is gorgeous?" Then she spoke again and her voice was soft and almost seductive. "Everyone needs to be touched sometimes princess and since we're here together why don't we help each other take some of the emptiness away?"

Part of Alicia felt repelled and wanted to push Kristen's hand away but something inside wouldn't let her.. "It's not the same."

Kristen's hand rested moved to the side of her face again and was rubbing up and down ever so softly. "I never said it would be, princess but it can still be something special if you let it. It's just between you and me and I know is different, but I will teach you, OK?"

Alicia's body shuddered and yet she knew if she was never going to be with a man anymore,it might be for the best. "You'll really teach me?" Alicia felt like she was at the edge of a precipice.

"We'll do it nice and slow and since we're probably gonna be here together for a long time we'll be able to learn together, right?"

Alicia fought the urge to tear up, because she knew that was taboo in here. "You know I've only been with a man, right?"

Kristen smiled. "That's the way it was with me, too. Like I said I'll teach you." As Kristen said that, her fingers were nimbly unbuttoning Alicia's blouse and Alicia did not resist.

Alicia's breathing got heavier as one button after another was undone and after Kristen finished, she gently eased the flaps of the blouse to the left and right to expose Alicia's stomach and breasts. "That wasn't hard, was it?" Alicia shook her head nervously. "Just relax. You have a beautiful young body, Alicia." Kristen's left hand cupped Alicia's left breast and Alicia responded with a soft moan. "Mmmm, I could tell from watching that they are perfect. We're going to get all that tension out and forget about everything for a little while, OK?"

"I'm still nervous."

"It's OK, just let the sensation carry you."

Alicia looked down as Kristen's right hand did the same with her right breast and her touch was so gentle as she alternatively squeezed but then used a velvety feathering touch. Alicia groaned and said: "Oh Gawd that feels good."

"This first time,it's going to be all just for you, princess. Aren't you feeling better already?" Alicia nodded while Kristen placed a hand under Alicia's left knee and bent it and then did the same on the right before lowering her head between Alicia's legs and as Kristen's tongue found its target Alicia let out a very soft but long moan.

"Oh..oh...oh..."

Kristen stopped for a second. "That's it focus on what I'm doing and how it feels and let your body go."

Alicia could vividly remember how Kristen's tongue and then her fingers continued their work there and Alicia was feeling waves and waves of pleasure overcoming her. By the time Kristen was done Alicia's body felt a tingling shivering electric feeling she had not felt since her last time with Peter and never could have imagined coming from another woman. Not only that, but for the time Kristen was doing it with her, the walls seem to fall away and the barrier between them vanished and was replaced by a warm fuzzy feeling she experienced when she had the sense of actually belonging to someone else, even as she was wishing it could have been Peter instead.

Kristen only had to do this a couple of more times and also showed her differing positions that allowed them to grind together as well before Alicia felt confident enough to reciprocate and pleasure Kristen's desirable, responsive, and appreciative body and Alicia even wondered if Kristen had met Peter first who would he have chosen. Surprisingly to Alicia she became excited when Kristen began to respond to Alicia's mouth, tongue and hands and it seemed to motivate her to try even harder to satisfy

Kristen so that she could see and feel her writhe and moan. It ended up that their sessions always seemed to end with their favorite 69 position. There was something about the totally mutual and open way they were able to satisfy each other's hunger that made Alicia understand that somehow they had formed a special bond with each other in this terrible place and even on nights when they did not make love, they would always find the time to just either spoon and cuddle or share long and passionate kisses.

Yet, after each time it was over, there was still something incomplete about it because Alicia knew there was nothing like the feel and touch of a man, and with each and every passing day she never lost the deep craving to have one in her life once again and all she could do to suppress it was to become more eager to let her mind go blank and allow her body to fully experience the pleasure that Kristen's touch and tongue always seemed to bring her even if there were times when she could just imagine that she was still with Peter, or expend all that energy to bring Kristen to multiple orgasms.

It was always Kristen who decided when they would make love. It was probably about twice a week now, and she had a private code with her. During dinner, Kristen would ask Alicia almost in a whisper: "So are you going to be my princess again tonight?" Alicia would always blush and nod her head.

As she was touching herself now,though her thoughts
were about Peter who always knew how to totally satisfy her, and
as she thought of the ways he did so her hand was moving slowly,
but steadily, because she wanted this to last.

She remembered that first meeting with him as she was in
the bar and waited for him to go over to the pool table and that
gave her the chance to talk to him. Even now she could still recall
the light musky scent his body gave off as she was close to him
and when he smiled his teeth were so white and perfect, and his
dark blond hair seemed to almost beg for her fingers to run
through it and when he looked at her, his dark blue eyes seemed
so sensitive, yet strong and intelligent.

Those visions made her moan "Oh Peter...." while she lay
on the bunk as her fingers massaged her clit and began to give
one of the moments of bliss that she could have here "....you were
so perfect, why did this have to happen?"

Yes there was the date for the movie, and then another
date that ended up at his place, a glass of wine together, and then
another, because this time she had told Mum she might be late
coming home. They were on the couch and laughing about
something and she "accidentally" spilled some of the wine on her
blouse. As these moments were replaying in her mind, her fingers
were going in and out of soaking wet pussy and making her
tremble and shiver in excitement.

23

"Oh I'm so sorry" Peter said.

"It's OK."

"It looks expensive hope it isn't ruined."

She smiled at him. "If you kiss me nicely, I'm wiling to forgive."

"I've been wanting to kiss you from the moment I saw you." As he said that, he leaned over and his lips met here. As they touched, Alicia remembered the way her body seemed to shiver and though he started slowly, she put her arms around him and pulled him closer and it was as if something was unleashed inside her and her lips hungrily pushed onto his and their tongues swirled around each other and that currently her fingers were deftly making her feel the same rising level of arousal..

She moaned even more as her fingers worked even faster while remembered feeling Peter's strong and skillful hands begin to explore her body and as she did remembered all this her other hand reached under the uniform and massaged and touched her left breast and then the right but it could never equal the special way that Peter used to do it.

The memories flooded back again as she could almost feel him touch her that night and it was like her clothes had seemed to remove themselves as she became eagerly naked for him while he did the same.

Her fingers were massaging her pussy feverishly now as

24

she remembered the way he picked her up off the couch and carried her into the bedroom and as he laid her down on that big, soft bed, his mouth covered one of her breasts as his hand reached down there. Before long, his mouth was at her pussy as well, and his tongue was licking and darting in and out of her and she was moaning and almost screaming. She could almost feel it again as he hand moved faster and also went in and out and her moans got louder. "Oh yes...yes..."

It was the same thing she said way back then and then as he got on top of her she eagerly spread her legs to invite him in but before he did he offered his manhood to her mouth and she sucked on it and tasted the slightly salty taste that told her that he was almost ready, so that when he took it down to its intended place he was already moistened but she knew that she was also already dripping wet.

"Mmmmm..mmmmm Peter...so good it's what makes life so special" Yes she was on her bunk and could feel the wetness against her fingers now and her hips were now humping up and down and gyrating and she knew she was close so very, very close.

That first night she had gasped as he entered her for that very special first time and it felt like she was going to melt. Her legs wrapped around him so that he would never leave and drew him deep inside her. Oh how she yearned for that feeling of having a man inside her again and she had thrust her hips up to greet him then and and once he was inside, he began to thrust, and soon the room was filled with the delicious sound of the light wet slapping and thumping noise as the bed slightly shook and then she could feel him going faster and she met his pace. Oh how it seemed to make her so hungry for him and she wanted all of him and even as he gave her one thrust she wanted another and another.

But he wasn't there and instead her moaning began to fill the cell, because this was more intense than the more recent times. "Uhhhhh uhhhhhhhh uhhhhh AHHHHHHHHHH!" Her body exploded and went wildly out of control as she had an orgasm just as she had that very first time with him. "MMMMMMMM" as images filled her mind in those seconds, the 3 month courtship that followed, the quiet wedding and the following wonderful three years, two months and five days that followed where it seemed Peter and her couldn't get enough of each other.

She opened her eyes and realized that she was panting. She looked over at Kristen's bunk and she was laying there and seemed still, but Alicia knew she had to be awake.

Alicia knew why this time it was so intense and seemed almost real. Her Mum had died and she'd been able to wheedle a compassionate one night leave and she knew by the next night she would actually be with Peter at his house. Alex had called Alicia into the office and informed her that the final arrangements had been made, but also warned her that Peter seemed like he was a reluctant host. Alex also explained that this was a highly unusual step and risky for her, and that the ankle bracelet would be very closely monitored and if it ever detected her outside Peter's house a squad car would be there almost instantaneously and whisk her back immediately to the facility.

She recalled Alex looking across the desk and felt the eyes piercing into her. "You understand how rare such a leave is for a natural life convict, don't you?"

"Yes Ma'am." Alicia answered. She had learned very quickly how to ingratiate herself to figures of authority in here.

"You also understand how unorthodox it is to allow you to be with a civilian alone, and a man to boot?"

"Yes Ma'am."

"You've been here long enough to know every favor has a price, doesn't it?"

Alicia looked down. "Yes Ma'am."

"So you also remember what I expect from you when you get back, don't you?"

Alicia took a deep breath. "Yes Ma'am. I'll be a good girl"

"Yes, a VERY good girl. Now back to your cell."

Her recollections of her meeting with Alex were

interrupted by the presence of Kristen at her bunk side and Kristen was grinning. "That was really an intense one, Alicia."

Alicia looked up and blushed as Kristen was gazing down at her and her long blond hair was at her shoulders. If she was free, even at 36 she'd still turn heads in a bar. "Yeah I guess it was intense."

Kristen sat down on the bunk next to Alicia. "I guess I should have suggested that you be my princess tonight." Yes there was that hard expression outside, but in here alone it was different, as after seven years they learned to do what you could almost never do in a maximum security prison; trust each other. Then her voice got playful. "I know why it was so intense." Kristen's hand reached over and stroked Alicia's hair. "Is it true what I heard through the grapevine?"

By now Alicia had learned to accept Kristen's small displays of affection. "What did you hear?"

Kristen caressed the side of Alicia face now. "You don't have to play dumb with me, princess. I know part of the leave involves you being alone with a man all night."

"How did you find out?"

"The walls have ears in this fucking place, my little princess."

"It's not just a man, it'll be Peter."

Kristen almost giggled. "That Peter? Soooo that's why you

28

were so excited!"

"Yeah it's been seven years since I seen him. It's been so long...."

Kristen replied. "After eleven years in this place I know all about long, princess. I thought you said he hates your guts."

Alicia leaned into her hand. "Yeah he says that, but when I'm there...."

Kristen continued stroking Alicia's hair gently. "After seven years I can appreciate how good you are in the sack but you said he hates you so don't get your hopes up, OK?" As she said that she planted a small kiss on Alicia's cheek. "I don't want to see you hurt."

"He still was willing to let them send me there."

"If something happens, great,but don't get your hopes up."

'It will go well. I know it." Right after Alicia said that, her lips came to met Kristen's and they began to kiss.

Kristen's hands went under Alicia's top and cupped her right breast. "When you get back, I'll remind you right away that you'll always be my princess. I do want it to be as you hoped for you, Alicia."

"MMMMM that always feels so good Kristen. At least you taught me some things that will help me with Peter. "

'When we're together you're still thinking of him aren't you?"

Alicia looked away as Kristen's hand on her breast made her let out a soft moan. "Are you upset with me, Kristen?"

"Fuck no. If I had the chance to have a man again I'd jump at it!" Then she grinned as she then stroked Alicia along her inside thighs. "This is different, but it's still good isn't it?"

"Alicia moaned as she felt Kristen's caress. "Yeah very good...." she felt Kristen's hand so light it was almost tickling her flesh now and causing goosebumps to form as she continued "....and special in its own way and yeah it gets me really wet."

Kristen continued stroking Alicia's thighs and made her squirm. "Yeah I sure know what my princess is like when she gets all wet, don't I?" Kristen grinned as she continued. "Well when you get back here I gotta hear all about it, every delectable second of it and then we're both gonna do some really hot stuff right?"

Alicia smiled "Steaming hot, Kristen."

Right now, however, tomorrow night was the entire focus of her life and thoughts now. She knew Kristen was right and that her hopes for that night with Peter might be dashed. However, even if they weren't, Alicia always understood once it was behind her, there was another, permanent life waiting for her back here and and that she needed to reconcile herself to it. In that life Alicia knew Kristen was going to play a central part of it as they aged together during the years ahead in the same cell.

However, that was two days away. In the immediate future, if she was fortunate, she still would have a chance to enjoy one special night with Peter and no matter what might happen afterward nobody could take that memory away from her of being a woman making love to her man.

Alicia and Kristen exchanged a lingering kiss after they spoke and both of them knew that it conveyed an understanding that when Alicia returned in two days she would no longer be distracted by the past and thoughts of Peter and then truly be Kristen's princess.

Chapter 4

Regrets and Plans

That night, Peter tidied up the house and also prepared the spare bedroom for Alicia and as he did, his mind wandered back over that period in his life. He had been struggling over the last seven years to put all of this behind him, but something always seem to open up the scar again and now this episode made him seethe with even more anger towards Alicia.

How dare she suggest his home as a place to stay? Who authorized this nonsense? She was a fucking murderer for crying out loud and they are letting her out for a damned funeral? So now it meant that the Townsend's had decided that Mikey and Alan couldn't attend their grandmother's funeral. The usual selfish Alicia at it again.

It had been a three month ordeal that started just before their three year wedding anniversary. Until then it had been like a dream. The boys loved Peter, and he was so much in love with Alicia and by the way she acted in the bedroom, he knew it was totally mutual, or so he thought.

He started to notice Alicia would seem distracted sometimes and when he asked her she just shrugged and just said she was distracted sometimes about some stuff and didn't want to talk about it.

One day, Mrs. Townsend called him and asked him to come over to their house to talk about something.

"Why don't I have Alicia and the boys come, too. That might be fun?"

"We just need to talk to you, Peter, if you don't mind."

"Sounds serious."

"How about tomorrow night?" When Peter agreed the phone went dead. Just then Alicia came out from the kitchen. "Who was that?"

Peter had never lied to her before but knew he had to. "Oh it was my boss. He needs me to work late tomorrow so I won't be home until later."

She put her arms around him. "I don't know if I can bear being apart that long, but yeah go ahead." They shared a passionate kiss and then that night was another of those nights that he could still recall even if they repelled him now. Even now, he knew that he'd never experienced the total exuberance and lack of inhibition that Alicia displayed in bed.

Peter drove to the Townsend's' house that was located in a dead end road in a respectable but modest development of single family homes. He was still in his uniform then and rang the bell and Mrs. Townsend answered it.

"Thanks for coming. How are Mikey and Alan doing?"

33

"Oh they're great. I'm sure Alicia will tuck them in nicely before I get home, but Alan thinks he's getting too old for that."

She didn't react, but ushered me into the living room where Mr. Townsend and their daughter Rachael was also sitting. "Wow is this a family pow wow?"

Mr. Townsend responded. "You could say that. We know that you met Alicia well after Jake died so we know you're totally innocent of anything."

"Innocent of what?'

"Jake's murder."

"What are you talking about. It was an accident....." I paused "wasn't it?"

Mrs. Townsend replied. "We all thought so, but something didn't seem right. He was a good driver and then to just drive into another lane? Then some things Alicia said didn't make sense either."

"Alicia? What does she have to do with it?"

Mr. Townsend responded. "She killed him, Peter. We have evidence. We got Jake's body exhumed and they found poison in his system and it had been in his system for only a few hours so he ingested it that night. They say he was rendered unconscious at the time the truck left the lane. Only someone with him that night could have given it to him."

"Why didn't they test him after the accident?"

34

'They did for alcohol or narcotics, never looked for this substance."

'I don't believe it I'm sorry. Alicia would never do something like that."

"It was almost perfect, Peter. Towards the end, we knew Alicia wasn't happy with him and always complaining about him. After Jake died it seems all she wanted was for us to be babysitters so she could go out to bars. I'm telling you she sure didn't act very sorry Jake got killed.

"Well maybe..."

"Then when we got the toxicology back we asked her if she ever took that medicine and then she actually went to local store and offered one of the clerks five thousand dollars to destroy the records of her prescription."

"So he didn't do that?"

"Oh he took the money but it seemed suspicious to him and he called the police and turned the money over to them. That drug is federally regulated and it's a crime to destroy records about purchases."

"Hasn't she been acting strange recently, Peter?"

"Well she's been a bit distracted."

"Just warning you, she's probably going to be arrested tomorrow or the next day at the latest."

"My God, what's going to happen with the kids?"

35

"They can stay with us."

"But their school, their friends..."

"It'll be a circus there, they need sanctuary. We need one thing, though, Peter just to wrap it up and maybe if it isn't there we were wrong."

"One thing?"

"Yes, Jake said one time that Alicia used to keep a diary. If you found it there might be something there to clear things up."

"So if I look and don't find it, or if it shows that she's innocent you're willing to take another look at all this and maybe clear her?"

"That's a possibility, Peter. Will you look?"

"Sure I'll look because I know she couldn't do something like this."

"Be careful. If we're right, Alicia is very dangerous, especially if she feels cornered."

"She's not dangerous. I know her."

"I hope you're right."

As Peter drove home he felt as if he had just been thrown off a cliff. He felt the tears in his eyes. She couldn't be capable of doing this.

That night he walked in the door and Alicia was waiting in a baby doll outfit. "It sucked you had to work late, Sweetie. Thought after a long day maybe I can relax you."

Oh she looked so good in that outfit. "Where are Mikey and Alan?"

"I tucked them in though Alan was a bit of a puke, he's sometimes so much like his father was."

"So Jake was a puke?"

She caught herself and laughed. "Oh just sometimes. Sweet man." Then she walked over to him and put her arms around him. "But not as sexy and exciting as you. How about a nice gentle massage followed by you know what?"

He smiled. "Tell you what, why don't you let me go upstairs and change and wait for me down here so we can have a glass of wine together first."

"I can bring it up with us."

He already felt the familiar stirring. "I'll be nicer down here then we can go up, baby."

She frowned. "Well OK, but don't you take too long."

She released him and he turned around and started up towards the stairs as he went towards the their. As he opened the door he turned back to make sure Alicia was remaining downstairs as he went in. He felt guilty because he did in fact see some massage oil on the night table as she had said she was going to do. She really did give wonderful massages.

First he did take a casual pair of slacks and shirt and throw them on after discarding his work clothes. He looked over at her dresser and went immediately to the bottom drawer and rummaged through the contents and at the bottom found a diary. He quickly went to the time frame and was reading and and felt his heart sink as he then heard a noise and quickly closed the drawer just before she walked in. She turned her head. "Were you looking for something, Sweetie?"

"Uh..well thought you might need a robe."

She grinned. "I hang them up in the bathroom."

"Oh." He lamely went in and took one off the hook and handed it to her.

"So while we're here you want that massage?"

After what he read he wasn't in the mood anymore for that. "I just remembered that I left something from work in the car."

"Oh Sweetie. Can't it wait?"

"No too sensitive to leave there."

She put her arms around him. "Does that mean afterward you're ready for that massage?" He felt his body about to shiver. 'What's wrong, honey? You're shaking."

"Nothing. Let's go back downstairs."

"You sure everything's OK,Sweetie?."

"Sure it's fine."

Just then her expression got serious and her grip tightened. "What were you looking for in there, anyway."

"Alicia just let it go, OK?"

"Where were you really tonight, Peter."

He tried to avert her gaze. "What are you talking about.? I told you it was a work meeting."

Suddenly her voice got hard and he'd never heard her sound like this before. "You're a shitty liar, anyone ever tell you that?"

"Does that mean you're a good one Alicia?"

Her eyes glared at him as she raised her hand as if to slap his face. He caught the hand before the blow could land. "You bastard!"

"Is that what you called Jake, too."

"You don't know shit about what it was like with Jake." Then her expression changed again to the Alicia he knew. "I'm sorry Peter, I know you aren't a bastard. Let's go downstairs and have some wine and then I'll give you one of those nice sensuous massages and then make love all night."

"So you're not upset with me, baby?"

"Oh I can see you're tired, so why not just have a drink and then we can go upstairs."

For the first time in his life, Peter felt a total and complete sense of fear. He couldn't leave because then he knew she'd dispose of the diary before the cops came. If he stayed, what would she do. He remembered Mr. Townsend's admonition that she was now dangerous. That's when he decided what to say: "Let me get that thing out of the car. I'll just get it and be right in.

"Yeah alright but this time don't keep me waiting so long."

Peter went out to his car and opened the door and as he did he saw a manual on the seat that he picked up. He also took his cell phone out and ducked down to call the Townsend's.

"Hello."

"It's Peter. I found it in her dresser. You were right."

"You alright?"

"No I'm not and she suspects something. You better act fast."

"I'll make a call just stall her."

"One thing I ask. When they come give her a chance to change she's in a nightie now and have them pull up quietly, no sirens or lights, OK?"

"Will do." He looked up and she was at the door looking out. So he brandished the manual. "There got it."

"Well the rest of the night will be much more fun. I already made a drink for you, honey."

'Hey I gotta go over this manual so why don't you go up and I'll join you later."

She pouted. "You've really started to get stinky. At least have the drink."

40

"Sure. Just leave it for me and I'll gulp it while I read."

"It's on the living room table. I'll bring mine up and remember you got a nice soothing massage waiting for you."

He went to the living room and saw the crystal wine glass filled with red wine and sat on the couch. He was able to watch through the front window and in about twenty minutes saw a slight movement outside. He walked briskly to the front door and quietly opened it to reveal a uniformed officer and two detectives.

"Is Alicia Lowry here?"

"She's upstairs last room on the left. We have two boys in the other rooms. She'll be allowed to change, right?"

"I'm Detective Galway,. Thank you for your cooperation. I assume we have your permission to search? "

"Yes the diary is in the bottom drawer of her dresser, the one on the left." The detective spoke to the officer. "When we're in there, take it, and bag it." The officer nodded . Then Detective Galway said: "Yeah sure, she can change before we take her to the station."

Detective Galway and the other detective started trudging up the stairs. Peter heard Alicia's voice. "Peter is that you?" There was no response as they disappeared and as they did Peter began to sob, and went upstairs because he was sure the commotion might wake up the boys.

"Who the hell are you?"

"I'm Detective Galway and this is Detective Osborne and Alicia Lowry we have a warrant for your arrest for first degree murder."

"No!! NO!! "

Just then he heard the other detective reciting the warning and her response. "Yeah I sure do want a fucking lawyer. How dare you come in here1"

"You are coming with us, and you can come dressed like that or you can have the chance to change into something more appropriate."

"And you're going to fucking watch?"

"You can go like that if you want."

"Fine get your jollies, but I'll have your damned badges before this is done."

Peter could hear the rustling of clothing and then silence and in a few more minutes after that Alicia emerged with her hands cuffed behind her.

When Alicia saw Peter she glared at him. "You knew about this you bastard, you let them in!"

As Detective Galway approached, he said :"Was that wine intended for you?" Peter nodded. "Might be a good idea to get it tested."

Alicia started agitating. "NO! NOOOO!"

Peter looked at the detective. "Please get that glass and her out of here! I didn't touch it so there should only have her fingerprints on it."

As Alicia was being hustled down the stairs into the awaiting police car Detective Galway said "Smart man Mr. Lowry. I'm sorry this had to happen." Then he called out. To the other detective "Get her processed and we'll be along with the other evidence.

The next day the boys awoke. "Where's Mommy" Mikey asked.

Peter had to hold back the tears. "She had to go away."

"When will she be back Dada?"

He sighed. He hadn't wanted to be called Dad out of respect for Jake so they agreed on Dada. "I don't know Mikey, it might be a long time. Both of you are going to go visit your Grandma and grandpa for awhile until we learn more OK?"

They actually beamed.

Sure enough the report came back about the wine and it had the same poison that was in Jake Townsend's system and it was just another nail in her coffin because Peter was told the diary explicitly laid out all the planning that had gone into it.

Peter also learned from the detective that once confronted with all the evidence and especially the wine glass from the night of the arrest, she finally confessed.

Once the news hit it was a sensation because it had been

43

over four years since the murder and it was a cold case. Peter declined all interviews, during the next couple of months the prosecutors were mulling whether to seek the death penalty.

Mrs Townsend was all for it, and very adamant because she was so very bitter over what Alicia did and how she had so easily moved on with her life and seemingly profited from her son's death, though they did work out a way for what was left of the insurance money to go to the kids instead of being forfeited.

Peter had a frank talk with Mr. Townsend and Jake's sister. "She tried to kill me, too, but I don't want Mikey and Alan to lose their mother as well."

Jake's sister was seething. "Jake didn't deserve it, the bitch should die and there's no way those children should ever have anything to do with her again!."

Peter responded. "I agree, but if you seek death she'll insist on a trial and dredge all this up. How will that help Mikey and Alan?"

Mr. Townsend nodded. "We need closure Peter. If that creature will agree I say do it." He then looked at his wife and daughter. "Right?" They both folded their arms in front of them and Mr. Townsend repeated his question. 'Isn't Peter right about that?"

They made faces and nodded. Mrs. Townsend responded. "But she's getting off easy."

Peter responded. "Don't be so sure of that."

Then he recalled the last time he ever saw her, and it was a little over seven years ago. The only decent thing she ever did in this whole thing was to plead guilty instead of having a circus of a trial. He made one last visit to her at the jail while she was awaiting sentencing and she was sitting across from him separated by glass and they were using a phone to communicate. The first thing she told him was that she had decided to plea guilty, and Peter didn't let on that he already knew. He looked at her now without makeup on and in the orange jumpsuit and her hair was tied in a bundle behind her. She looked tired and a little worn and already looked like a convict and now even a little older than she seemed just a couple of months ago on the night of her arrest.

He remembered her saying tearfully after she told him of her plea. "You know my lawyer says it's probably going to get what they call total life, no parole."

His reply was cold. "Probably? It will Alicia. They had you dead to rights."

He saw anger flash momentarily across her face as she said "Yeah thanks to that damn busy body.!" Then it was like she caught herself again. "At least I'll spared the kids and those people going through a trial. Isn't that worth something, Peter?"

He looked at her. He knew she really pled to spare her

miserable life, but why waste his breath saying that he knew "It was the least you could do. By the way I filed divorce papers a couple of days ago. You should get them soon enough."

He remembered seeing the tears begin to flow. Once that would have made him want to hold her but now he was unmoved. "Do you have to do that right now?"

"Did you cry as much at Jake's funeral Alicia? Would you have also cried at my funeral? How real are they?"

"Please, except for Mum it means I'll be all alone!"

"You should have thought about that before. I've got a life to live and I'm not going to have it tied up with someone who tried to kill me and who is going to be locked up forever. "

"Tried to kill you?"

"Don't act dumb."

He never forgot the way she instantly composed herself and lifted her head totally up. "So that's what you really want a divorce?"

"Yes Alicia, that's what I want."

"Then make yourself happy." He thought he saw Alicia's eyes get teary again.

"I'll sure be happier after the divorce Alicia." He got up and started walking to the door.

"Please can't you stay and let me explain?"

He looked back. "Goodbye Alicia. Nobody is more suited

to be in prison than you." He never looked back as he left the room and walked briskly to the door.

So the Alan's old bedroom was made up, he arranged to leave work early tomorrow so he could eat early before they dropped her off.

Oh damn he was thinking. If he could be doing anything else in the entire world than this tomorrow he'd volunteer.

Chapter 5

Not The Usual Day

Alicia had gone back to sleep but as always everyone was awakened at 6am for roll call. She and Kristen stood outside their cells while the officers went by and counted and after several minutes they were dismissed.

Kristen was assigned to the laundry while Alicia had a job in the kitchen to get breakfast ready at 7am.Unlike tonight, Alicia wanted the day to go quickly. She knew that she would be taken to Alex's office at 3:00pm, and the processing for the leave would occur.

She was eagerly contemplating the procedure where the ankle bracelet would be placed on her and then she could shower alone and then change into civilian clothes. She smiled because that outfit she wore at sentencing was still in storage, and she'd wear that. It was well cut and smart and Peter would know immediately that she was still the same desirable woman she was seven years ago. There was a mirror in the cell and she looked once again at the face that stared back. In her uniform and her icy, hard expression the image that reflected back to her was that of a convict. Once she left here, that would need to change tonight. The clothes would help, and Alex said she could use makeup as well.

She's still be the woman he married, maybe a little older, but not yet too old. She wondered what he looked like now. Was there any graying of the hair? Had he kept in shape, and still have those wonderful tight pecs and slim muscular thighs and muscular firm stomach or had he aged and gained weight and gone soft like some men do as they age? It didn't matter, because he'd always be what she imagined, and she was certain that one thing would be the same and it would be that awesome cock that always seemed to find the right spot inside her and make her scream out in totally blissful ecstasy.

She shook off the thoughts and went over to the kitchen. "Lowry, your late!" Beatrice, the convict who ran the kitchen glared at her. She was stout and probably in her fifties with graying hair and had been inside for over fifteen years now.

"Sorry Beatrice."

"Get your ass over and start on the eggs!" Alicia nodded and went over and took out the mixture they used for the scrambled eggs. "For that you'll be expected to wipe down the tables as well."

Normally she'd say something but Alicia didn't want to rock the boat today. "OK."

Soon the other convicts were lining up for their meals and as thy shuffled in, she spooned out some eggs and when she saw Kristen in the line Alicia smiled and gave her a little extra.

After their meal the kitchen staff got to eat and then it was time to clean up. As Alicia was finishing scrubbing the pots before going over to the tables, Beatrice came quietly next to her.

"Don't think I didn't hear about you getting to get out tonight to go to your Mom's funeral tomorrow. Also heard that you're going some place tonight and some man is gonna own that pussy of yours all night isn't he?"

"What of it?"

"So what did you have to do for someone for a single night of fucking?"

Alicia closed her eyes. It truly had gotten out. "What does it matter to you? You're just jealous that's all because no man would have you!"

Beatrice grabbed Alicia's shoulders and pulled her close. "Jealous, huh? You think no man would have me, bitch! I was once young and pretty like you and had any man I wanted though they were all worthless bastards! No man would have me, huh? Just remember when you look at the way I look you're looking at your future, bitch!"

Alicia gave Beatrice a slight shove to push her away and made sure she gazed at her with the hardest coldest look she could muster. "So while I look like this I shouldn't try to be with a man? You would have done the same."

"Yeah right a man who just wants a nice piece of ass. I'll

make sure you have lots of fun here in the kitchen when you get back, understand?"

Alicia broke out in her best sneer. "I don't give a shit what you do, because when you do you'll still know I got what you never got." Alicia then grabbed the rag and went over and wiped the tables, put the supplies away and then went back to her cell.

Kristen was not back since the work at the laundry was longer, though she made more for her commissary account. Alicia laid on her bunk and closed her eyes and began to think of tonight. Wearing actual clothes and makeup again. Being with Peter and if things went really right making the night so very, very special. She was always good at attracting men, somehow in high school they flocked around her but she had made a bad choice the first time with Jake but not the second with Peter. Oh why did Peter have to hate her so much?

About half an hour later Kristen walked back to the cell. At least during the day the cell door was left open so they were free to wander in the block though too much wandering could lead to trouble.

Kristen sat on her bunk cross legged. "So when do you start getting ready?"

"I should be called to Ms. Foreman's office around three o'clock."

"Guess it's a dumb thing to say, but I wish I could be

there, too."

"Yeah that bitch Beatrice in the kitchen knows and gave me shit about it."

Kristen laughed. "Yeah she despises anyone who is pretty." Then she paused for a moment."I was once in the office and her file was open. I can see why, she was once a high price hooker and quite a looker."

"Beatrice? You're kidding."

"Yeah killed one of her clients when he tried to stiff her and been in here almost thirty years."

Alicia thought of her words that must have stung. "Well the way she was so shitty I gave it back to her."

Kristen replied. "Rolls right off her back. Don't sweat it."

Alicia spent the rest of the morning laying on the cot and reading. It was a romance novel and she was able to occasionally close her eyes and escape and imagining herself as the heroine in it. Had it been more private, she would have been tempted to touch herself but kept her control.

Eleven thirty came and it was time to go to the kitchen again to prepare lunch. This time it was Mac and Cheese and the cleanup was a bit messy, but at least this time she didn't have to wipe tables. As Alicia finished up she saw Beatrice over by the sink finishing a small task and so she went over because she remembered one rule. Don't make enemies if you don't have to. "I shouldn't have said what I said to you, Beatrice."

She looked up sternly. "What should you have not said?"

"Pretty much everything."

Her expression softened. "So you were finally wrong about something."

"Wrong enough about a few things because I ended up in here."

She smiled. "Yeah but somehow smart enough when your Mom croaked to manage to be with a man. You don't give a shit about your Mom, you just want some guy's cock in that pussy of yours don't you?"

"I did love my Mum." She hesitated as Beatrice glared at her. Then Alicia got that hard look again. "Yeah but you can't blame me for wanting to get fucked, can you?"

Beatrice nodded. "Yeah you got me, I do envy you." Her expression seemed to soften a bit. "Well, well so you're not as dumb as you act sometimes. So it's gonna be take what he will give you and give him as little as possible in return, right?"

Alicia responded. "That's right. That love stuff is for suckers. I knew him from before and he's good enough in the bedroom and that's all I care about."

Beatrice cocked her head. "Maybe I was wrong about you, sugar. Forget what I said before about what's waiting for you when you get back, you'll be fine."

As Alicia went back to her cell she knew that what she said to Beatrice should be her attitude because Peter's love had long since gone. Her approach would be based purely on physical seduction and attraction so that he would be aroused enough to go to bed with her. She knew what he liked, how he reacted, and what special touches especially excited him. That's what she had been planning over the last few days in her head. She just needed the chance to be able to reach him, a few touches and words and hopefully he'd be putty in her hands like he was during their marriage,and yet she still hoped it would be more than that. She closed her eyes, and knew that what made his caresses and lovemaking so special was that she knew there was love behind it and as she surrendered to him, she knew it was because she desperately needed to share her body with him,and no matter what she had told Beatrice, she knew she still felt the same way now.

A little before three o'clock a guard was at Alicia's cell. "You need to come with me because you're going to Ms. Foreman's office."

Alicia nodded and got off her bunk. Before she left, Kristen went over and hugged her and whispered :"Good luck tonight. I envy you."

Alicia planted a small kiss on Kristen's cheek and said "I wish you could do something like this,too."

Alicia and the guard walked down the hall and after a barrier was unlocked with the distinctive buzz,she was led through another corridor and then ushered into Alex's office.

"Sit down, Alicia. I need you to sign some paperwork before we can proceed with the leave." Alicia dutifully sat on the other side of the desk and Alex pushed two forms in front of her. "The first form is for the leave itself, and authorizes the monitoring device and agreeing that any attempt to leave the premises where you are left will constitute escape. If you agree,you may sign it."

It was probably the first thing she had signed in seven years, and she glanced at it and then quickly signed it. "Good girl. Now the second form is what we discussed earlier and states that after your return after the leave,you consent to your placement into a special unit for one day a week. You know what that means,don't you?"

"Yes Ma'am. It means I'll need to be a good girl for you. "

"Yes a very good girl for me. If you want the leave go ahead and sign it." Alicia gave the form a very slight glance and signed it. Alex took the forms from the desk and placed them in a folder. "Thank you Alicia. I know you're anxious about doing that special unit, but I can assure you that you will learn quickly how to please me there."

Alicia thought back to the meeting when the leave was

55

discussed and when she was told about the requirement that after she returned that she be transferred to this special unit. Alex even took her to the unit to show it to her. "Yes, when you get back,this is where you will be on those days. The room had a large bed, but also some sex toys and restraints. "This is where you will show me how a good girl behaves with me."

Her thoughts were interrupted by Alex. "Well, I have your outfit laid out in the bathroom, and why don't you go in there to shower, change and put on some makeup?"

Alicia smiled and gave her thanks and walked into the bathroom and sure enough on a counter was a pair of panties and her bra laid out quite neatly with a pair of navy blue pumps carefully placed on the floor in front of the counter.

Alex called out to her. "I made sure the outfit was cleaned and pressed for you and it stood up well over the years. It's still stylish as well. When you're done you can come out." That made Alicia look over to a hook on back of the door where her navy blue outfit was hung inside a clear plastic dry cleaning bag.

Alicia stripped down out of the jumpsuit and prison panties and shoes and put them in a pile against the wall and stood in front of the mirror totally naked to observe herself briefly. She smiled because she knew that she was still as attractive as she had been the last time Peter had seen her.

She closed the door and it was like being in another world

to be able to shower totally privately like she used to do. She saw that there was a switch for an exhaust fan and turned it on and from then on the whirring of the fan filled the room. After the water was turned on and ran to get to the right temperature,she stepped into the shower and after letting it wet her entire body and hairs she shampooed her hair and rinsed it and then put the conditioner on and let it set while she used the lavender bathing gel to soap her body. She had almost again forgotten how sensual a shower could be as she could smell the fragrance and take the time to savor the feel of her lubricated gelled hands roam over her body. It reminded her about how much of a sensual being she had always been although she had been forced to suppress those urges for the last seven years. Finally she had soaped all over her body that included her pussy and resisted the urge to stimulate herself because hopefully that night it would be done even more in a very special way. Then it was a matter of rinsing off the conditioner, stepping out of the shower, and drying herself off with an awaiting towel, that so unlike the prison towels was plush and deep. A hairdryer was also on the counter and she picked it up, plugged it in and turned it on and as she did the noise also filled the room as she separated her hair and dried it in stages.

When her hair was finally dried,she turned off the exhaust fan and picked up the pink lace panties and pulled them on, followed by the bra that pulled around her body backwards to connect it and then spun it around and then pulled the cups over her breasts. She'd almost forgotten how it felt to have a real properly fitting bra on again.

She got up off the toilet and opened the dry cleaning bad and unhooked the white blouse and put it on. As she did, she looked in the mirror and smiled because the Alicia Lowry that was once gone was beginning to reemerge before her very eyes. She buttoned the blouse and then reached for the skirt and stepped into it and pulled it up and zipped it up the back and felt for the button to attach it. As she did she was yearning for the moment she hoped to have Peter reversing this process. The jacket was next and when she put it on, her outfit was complete and as she looked again in the mirror she felt so good, but something was missing. She then saw the foundation and mascara and pale lipstick on the sink and knew that's what it was, so she applied it and then when she looked again she knew that the transformation had been complete. Staring back at her was someone she knew, and had missed terribly and then she opened the bathroom door and stepped out.

"I want to thank you, Ma'am. Thank you so very much."

"I'm sure that's what your mother would have wanted for tomorrow."

For the first time in prison Alicia allowed the tears to swell up in her eyes. "Yes, Mum always wanted me to look

58

pretty."

Alex said: "Well something is still missing. Turn around."
Alicia obeyed and felt Alex's hands reach around her chest and
then pull up and realized she was putting something on her. It was
a string of pearls and then she also gave Alicia a pair of earrings
to match. "There now you can look and see what you think."

She looked in the mirror and finally saw that she was like
a real woman again. "Thank you Ma'am, than you so much."

"Here's the matching purse as well, so you look
complete." It was a cream white small bag. "Since I've been so
nice to you for this you'll be ready to be a good little girl when
you get back, won't you?" Alicia nodded.

"One last thing of course." Alex held up the ankle
bracelet. "Right or left leg, your choice."

"Left."

Alicia lifted her left ankle onto a chair and Alex carefully
placed it around it and clicked the bracelet. "Remember any effort
to remove it is instantly detected and will end this little adventure,
understand?"

"Yes Ma'am."

"Good your transport is ready so let's get you to a car.
Your host didn't want it to be conspicuous so it's one from our
regular fleet. No handcuffs or restraints and you can be in the
front seat as the agreement stated."

59

Alex accompanied Alicia down some stairs into a courtyard where a medium sized gray Ford was waiting. A man was standing next to the car.

"Liam, you understand the instructions and the destination is loaded in your GPS?"

"Yes Ma'am. Drop off at six thirty pm, pick up at nine am."

You'll have an extra hour so use the expense account for the two of you to have dinner first before drop off, since the host stated he wants to eat alone." Liam nodded. Alex then said: "See you tomorrow Alicia."

Liam was not very good at conversation and so for the most part they rode silently together as they went down the road. Soon Alicia began to see some familiar sights,although she also did notice some things had changed over seven years. She was relieved that Peter had chosen to stay in the same house they had shared together.

As they pulled into the town, Liam finally spoke a complete sentence. "It's five o'clock and Ms. Foreman said I was to have you eat before dropping you off. I looked up some places and so do you want American or Italian?"

"Do you like Italian, Liam?" Alicia asked.

"Sure why not? In that case we'll go to a place called Alfonso's."

"Mmmmm Alfonso's is good, at least it was."

Liam parked the car in the parking lot and got out and Alicia did the same while carrying her purse. Alicia remembered that she had once eaten there at least once a month and wondered if anyone would remember her after all this time. She realized that it would be better if they didn't but chose not to alert Liam of the possibility since she suddenly felt a craving to taste their food again. One thing was clear. When Alex had told Liam to have her eat and put it on the expense account, Liam wasn't going to scrimp on the cost.

Though she was more stylishly dressed than Liam, he was wearing an open collar shirt and sports jacket and dress slacks so he didn't look out of place.

They walked into the restaurant and Alicia recognized Rudolph right away in the front. Like those years ago, he had a smile on his face and spoke with a smooth slight Italian accent. "Good evening and welcome Sir and Madam. Are you here for dinner?"

She let Liam speak. "Yes sir, table for two."

He smiled., but there was no hint of recognition in his expression. "I'll put you somewhere quiet."

Much to her surprise, Rudolph placed them at was once her favorite table where she and Peter would sit when they came here. It was in the corner and away from the others. Maybe it was

61

indeed a good sign. Before Rudolph left he placed a menu in front of both of them.

The busboy came over and poured the water and brought rolls and butter. Alicia looked down and it was the first time in seven years that she could actually use real silverware, including a knife. Then the waiter came over and Alicia didn't recognize him.

"May I get you a drink to start?"

Before Liam could respond Alicia blurted out. "Yes I think I'll have a glass of Cabernet."

Liam glared at her but said nothing and that made Alicia smile inside. He muttered: "I'll just have coffee I have to drive."

Once the waiter left Liam leaned forward. "Ordering wine? What kind of stunt was that?"

"Did Ms. Foreman ever say I couldn't have one?"

Liam kept his voice down. "The rules state that inmates..."

Alicia cut him off. "I'm on leave, I'm not an inmate right now, and anyway do you really want to make a fuss over it?"

"Alright, but when we get back tomorrow I'll have a talk with Ms. Foreman about this."

"I don't care what she says tomorrow because I'm having the wine tonight. Anyway why don't you just enjoy your free dinner?"

The waiter brought the wine over and also poured Liam

the coffee. She lifted the glass tilted it to Liam. "Here's to a great dinner, Liam." He still had a bit of a glower as she took a sip and the thrill made her body shiver. She'd always loved to have a nice glass or two of wine with dinner and had missed it so.

He retorted. "Just one glass though."

She smiled. "Of course." They both looked at the menu. She looked up at Liam. "You know the veal is really good here."

"Veal, huh?" Her words made his sourness seem to go away and he smiled. "Thanks for the suggestion." As he spoke Alicia took one of the rolls and put it on her bread plate and broke a piece off and buttered it. Liam did the same. 'So you used to eat in places like this?"

"Yeah even here every month. This is reminding me of how much I miss it."

"You sure this leave was a good idea for you because of that?"

"Better to have something once more and miss it again then to never have it, right?"

"One way to look at it."

Liam ordered the Veal Parmigiana and Alicia ordered the Veal Romano, and each came with pasta. Alicia said: "You'll love the sauce. It's heavenly."

As they waited for the meal Liam asked: "It's none of my business, but how the hell did a lady like you end up like this?"

"Long story, Liam. I was young and made a bad choice and tried to get past it and thought I had but the law caught up to me."

"Obviously Ms. Foreman believed it was OK for you to do this,so I guess you can't be that bad."

"Yeah after this I'm probably in there forever."

"I'll be outside that house so don't try anything, understand?"

"Getting overtime for all this I hope."

He grinned. "Oh yeah big time."

"And a free meal, too. Don't suppose the company's too bad is it."

"I've had worse, and lots uglier."

"Gee thanks for the compliment." The meal came and in between sips of the wine Alicia ate her meal while Liam did between coffee sips and refills.

When the meal was done they declined dessert because the time was getting short and Liam settled up with a credit card and they left the restaurant. She gave it a last look before leaving and trying to soak in the experience just one more time.

 As they got in the car Lam asked :"It's six fifteen how close are we?"

"We might be early by a few minutes, but remembering Peter I'm sure he's prepared so it'll be OK."

64

They sat silently in the car again as Liam drove down familiar streets until they reached the house. She hadn't seen it since the night of her arrest. Alicia's palms got sweaty and her heart was racing as they parked out front. She did notice a car was parked in the driveway, so she knew he was home. "Before I can leave you alone, he'll have forms to sign." He reached back and took a clipboard from the rear seat. Then after he had it, both he and Alicia got out of the car and walked to the front door.

Chapter 6

Reunion and Confrontation

It only took a minute for the door to open. It was Peter who stood at the door. He was wearing a blue dress shirt and khaki slacks with loafers on. He was still trim and athletic and still with no gray hair as Alicia remembered him, and she couldn't help but take that first minute to feast her eyes on him.

Peter, on the other hand seemed to focus on Liam as he spoke to Peter. "I assume you're Mr. Lowry. I have some forms for you to assign before I can complete the transport."

Alicia couldn't help feeling like she was being treated as some cargo being delivered to its destination.

"What forms? Ms. Foreman never mentioned anything about any forms."

"Standard stuff. It just acknowledges your agreement that you are accepting custody of the prisoner until nine tomorrow morning."

"Fine. Do you have a pen?" Liam produced one together with the clipboard and Peter took the time to read the entire sheet carefully and then signed it. "Do I get a copy?"

"One underneath, Sir." Peter nodded, and opened the clip and took the bottom sheet. "I'll be here to collect her at nine sharp tomorrow morning." Then Liam turned to Alicia. "Make sure you are ready to go then."

"I will, Sir."

Liam responded. "If you need anything Mr. Lowry, or if there is any problem I've been instructed to remain out here so you can come right over"

Peter responded. "That will be quite uncomfortable. Would you like to stay inside with us?"

Alicia blanched. If he accepted all her plans would be ruined.

"It's OK. My days on the force I used to do stakeouts so I'm used to it. Anyway Ms. Foreman said I was to remain out here. I'll be fine."

After that exchange Liam went back to his car as Alicia walked inside while Peter closed the door behind her.

"Looks like you've taken care of yourself, Peter. You still look great."

"Thanks. You actually look good as well."

She felt something flutter inside her. "I really do?"

"Yes." Then his voice got very business like. "Now I did set up a room for you and I'll show you up there."

"You want to talk a little first?"

"I want to show you to your room, Alicia. There's nothing to talk about."

"The only person who seemed to care a shit about me has

just died and there's nothing to talk about. Don't you care at all?"

"Don't get me started, Alicia. I didn't want to do this but she was a decent lady and I know she would have wanted you at her funeral and I made sure you will be. You'll have Alan's old room."

"How are the boys?"

"You mean the sons of the man you murdered? They're doing alright with the Townsends."

"You ever see them? Talk to them?"

"Yeah as much as I can. You know where the room is."

Please, can't we just sit and talk over a glass of wine and be adults about this?"

"My days of getting a glass of wine from you ended seven years ago." Alicia blanched and started to tear up. "Please don't start turning on the faucets, Alicia. I'm not buying it."

"Don't you like my outfit? Don't you like the way I look? I wanted to look nice for you."

"Then you wasted your time. You fooled me all those years but you don't fool me now."

"Fooled you? How did I fool you. By loving you?"

"You never loved me! You loved money1"

"Peter, you don't understand!. I know I made a mistake."

"A mistake? A man died because of you."

Alicia looked down, and for the first time in over seven

years began to weep. "Yes he did. I was wrong. I'm paying for it every day, every single day."

"But you're still alive and he isn't."

"I can't bring him back and oh God every night I wish I could and go back but I can't. I tried every day when I was with you to somehow be different, be a good wife and mother to the boys, I was hoping, just hoping...."

"That you'd gotten away with it?"

"I had found a man I loved, and was so happy and wanted to please you so much. You don't know how much I love you and miss you...."

"Miss me? Love me? You poisoned my wine that night!"

"I realized you had taken their side against us Peter, I had to. Don't you understand?

'I'm supposed to understand?"

"I know you loved me once. Please can't you remember how you did. This is like a miracle, I've been given one last chance to be a woman again with a man I love before they take me back there forever. You don't know what it's like."

"So now your Mum dying was a miracle? I don't care what it's like!"

"You don't care that I've got nobody that cares about me anymore? You don't care that every day I get older and am just watching myself get older and soon I'm going to be an old woman alone and dying forgotten in prison? How can you be so heartless?”

“You really have to ask me that?”

“All I'm asking for in one night, one last night to be who I used to be. I know you loved being with me, and I made you feel special and I felt that way with you.” Alicia moved closer and put her arms around Peter who stiffened. She looked up at him and the tears were flowing down her cheeks. “Please Peter, please am I asking too much?”

He brusquely pulled her arms away from him. “Why would I want to do that? You disgust me, Alicia. You tried to kill me and then you ask me to make love to you?”

His words struck Alicia like a thunderbolt. “You keep saying I tried to kill you? Who said I tried to kill you?”

“You poisoned my wine. They told me that it was in that glass you wanted me to drink that night, so don't play dumb. I WANT YOU OUT OF MY SIGHT! I'll call you in the morning. Go now!”

“I DIDN'T TRY TO KILL YOU! They never told you it wasn't a large dose? I couldn't kill you, I just needed you to fall asleep so I could run. Peter, how could you ever believe I'd try to harm you?” She started to cry. “I can't believe the bastards never told you that.”

I'm supposed to believe someone who killed their first

husband that she didn't try to kill the second one when he was a threat? Just leave.!"

Alicia saw the darkness descending around her as she started to sob even more. "As you wish, Peter, I'll go. I really didn't try to kill you, maybe you don't believe me but it's God's honest truth. If I had, they would have charged me with attempted murder of you wouldn't they? Please think about that!"

As she said that the still sobbing Alicia ran upstairs and went into Alan's old room where there was a child's dresser and twin bed. She threw herself face down onto the bed and started to wail into the pillow. She had truly lost him and Kristen had been right and it didn't go well and all her hopes were for nothing. Now she'd have to endure what Alex had in mind for her without even a memory of a final blissful night here.

Peter was shaking as he watched Alicia run up the stairs. Even in his anger he still admired the way her body moved as she went up. He also had tears in his eyes that he only allowed to emerge when she had left the room.

We went into the kitchen and opened the refrigerator door and took out an opened bottle of Chardonnay and then poured himself a glass. Ever since that call from the prison he'd been drinking a bit more than he usually did. As he drank, he cursed Alicia more. Why did this all have to happen? It was like a festering sore in his soul. Yes he had loved her and as much as he had been trying no woman was ever like her and it made him hate her even more. As he sipped a nagging thought kept eating at him. Now that she had said it he began to wonder why didn't they also charge Alicia with attempted murder? Could she have been right? What if she was?

He remembered a business card that Detective Galway had given him after the arrest. He went into the desk in the study and opened the left drawer, and rummaged through the papers and it wasn't there. He went to the next drawer and there it was and a number was written on the back. He remembered the detective saying it was his home number, who knows if it was still good, but now Peter just had to know and so he picked up the phone on the desk and called.

It rang three times and someone answered.

"Is this Detective Galway?"

"It was but I'm retired now. Who is this?"

"Peter Lowry. Do you remember me?"

"Oh yes the Townsend murder case. You were quite a help."

"I have a question."

"Sure, I'll answer if I can."

"Why didn't she get charged with attempting to murder me?"

After Peter heard the answer, he slowly and sadly hung up

the phone and took another sip of his wine. He thought for another few minutes, especially about the way things had been for the last seven years. Maybe he did need to confront the ghosts of the past and finally exorcise the demon that seemed to rage inside him.

Peter walked into the kitchen, opened a cabinet and took out another wine glass and poured some of the Chardonnay into it and refreshed his glass as well and slowly walked up the stairs carrying both glasses.

Chapter 7

The Last Night

As he approached Alan's old room he could still hear sniffling because the door had been kept open. He tentatively called into her. "May I come in?"

Alicia looked up from the bed. "You know you can. It is your house. Are you here to tell me more about how horrible a person I am?" Then she noticed he was carrying the wine in his hands and then scrambled off the bed onto her feet. "Does the wine mean you changed your mind and we can at least talk?"

"I know you always liked Chardonnay and I'm sure you would love to have a chance to drink some before they send you back tomorrow."

She smiled and walked over and took the proffered glass from him. "A lot of things I'd love to sample before I do that. " She sipped from the glass. "MMMM that tastes sooo good Peter. Thank you."

He smiled as he patted her shoulder with his free hand. "All that from just one sip?"

"First sip in seven years,except for the Cabernet I managed to get at dinner tonight. Yes you knew how much I liked wine. What changed your mind about talking? "

"You made me curious so I called Detective Galway just

now."

"What did he say?"

Peter shook his head "Well he's retired now but he remembered the case. He said you must have screwed up because it wasn't a fatal dose, it only would have made me sleep for a few hours."

"He never told you sooner than this?"

"He said he told the Townsends and assumed they would tell me."

She held back the urge to sob or rage but remained cool. "I'm not surprised they held it back when they saw how much your assumption made you hate me. They wanted to make sure I lost everything "

"You did kill their son and for me it's normal to hate someone who you think was trying to kill you."

Alicia walked closer to him as she took another goods sip from the glass. "I could never kill you, Peter, and I wish you could have just known that. I loved you and I still do. I'm so sorry, so very, very sorry this all happened."

"I am angry at them. They had no right to withhold it from me. I'm sorry, too."

She walked closer to him and put her glass down on the dresser as Peter sat on the bed and still held his to take another sip "That's right they didn't, but I know that since I caused them so much pain, they would do anything to cause me pain, too.”

“You really understand that?”

She walked to where she was standing right in front of him as he sat on the side of the bed. “Well you always had a a way to bring out the best in me, Peter. I wish every day I could have changed things, but nothing can be done about that now.”

“You still put poison in my wine and wanted me to drink it, even if it wasn't a fatal dose. If you love me why did you do it?”

'I was scared. I didn't know what to do. I just knew had to get away because I just couldn't bear thinking of something like this happening to me, and I knew you'd try to stop me so I just needed time to run.”

“Do you have any idea how much pain and anger that caused me knowing you did that?”

“I'm sorry, Peter, I'm so sorry.”

“Maybe the Townsends got closure by seeing you put away, but I didn't.” As he said that, he carefully placed his glass next to hers on the night table.

“I'd do anything to make it up, I really would.”

“Well it's nothing like what happened for them, but this is going to be something even more personal.” As Peter said that,he grasped Alicia's wrist and pulled her to his right side and pulled her across his lap.

"Peter...what are you doing?"

"Going to let you know how much pain I was feeling these last seven years." He grasped the bottom of her skirt and pulled it up to her waist and saw her panties. "I see you never lost your taste for pink, have you?"

"Peter, I'm sorry."

"You'll be even sorrier. You wanted to talk? We'll talk when you're like this!" He pulled the panties down to her knees. "You deceive me and then try to poison me and you were supposed to love me?" SMACK SMACK SMACK SMACK!!

"OW!! OW!! It hurts!"

"That's right it hurts because I was hurt!" SMACK!! SMACK!!!!SMACK!!!SMACK!!! "So you wanted to be with me tonight? Well now you are!!" SMACK!!! SMACK!!! SMACK!!! SMACK!!!

"OW!! OW!!!"

"So I suppose you want me to stop?" SMACK!!! SMACK!!! SMACK!!! SMACK!!!

"OW!! Oh Peter, I didn't want to....no...no if it hurt I should hurt."

SMACK SMACK!! SMACK!!! Her bottom was turning more pink now. "You really understand that, Alicia?" SMACK SMACK SMACK

"OW OW Yes I hurt you hurt everyone I want it to really

hurt OWWW I deserve it!"

SMACK!!! SMACK!!! SMACK!!! SMACK!! The sound of hand striking bare flesh reverberated through the house. "Even if it's going to hurt even more?" SMACK SMACK SMACK!!!!

Alicia was sobbing. "Having you hate me hurt a lot more. If this will make you not hate me I want more, lots more!"

By now her butt was a deep pink and she was crying even more as Peter lifted his hand to strike her again he stopped. "I would have stood by you, Alicia. I would have."

Alicia's sobs were now getting gentle as she responded. "Stood by and watch me sent to prison for life like this? What kind of life would that be? I was afraid of prison, and now I know why. It's terrible, Peter."

Peter started rubbing Alicia's spanked bottom and suddenly his voice was soft, as if spanking her had begun to remove the demons that had been haunting him for seven years.. "It's been hard for you, hasn't it?"

Alicia started to sob on his lap as the pain she kept inside her for seven years finally flowed out of her. "Every day is the same. I wear the same ugly uniforms. I can't trust anyone, and never have any hope of something better or being with anyone that I can love or trust. Every day that passes makes me realize I'm getting older and older and that I'm going to turn into an old shriveled and used up woman with nothing to show for my life until I finally die in that place. Yeah not getting the death penalty means my body didn't die but it doesn't mean that I'm really living anymore."

Peter's right hand continued to rub her bottom and what she could not see was that Peter's eyes were still tearing."I don't know what I can do about it."

She looked back over her shoulder at him. "Could you at least forgive me? Please?"

Peter thought of the happier times, and those special moments they had shared before these events came to the surface as he gently rubbed her warmed bottom. "I can't overlook what you did to Jake, but yes, now I can forgive what you did to me."

Alicia broke into tears. "I was praying, hoping you would. If you need to spank me some more to show me how much I hurt you so that you forgive me that's what I want."

"That's what you really want, Alicia?"

She sniffled. "Yes make it hurt. Make it hurt bad."

Peter took deep breath and gazed down at Alicia's dark pink butt slightly squirming as it was perched on his lap and then he knew he really did need to make it hurt. Now he raised his hand high up and began to bring it up and down rapidly. SMACK!!! SMACK!!! SMACK!!! SMACK!!! SMACK!!! She began to cry again and it got loud as her legs began to kick, and yet he noticed that before each smack she slightly lifted her bottom up as if to accept the punishment. Her crying seemed to drive him to go even faster and harder. SMACK!! SMACK!!! SMACK!!! SMACK!!! SMACK!!! SMACK!!! SMACK!!

As Alicia felt his hand making the burning and stinging grow and make her cry, it seemed in that moment her entire being was consumed by it and yet she was comforted by the fact that it was him holding her in position. The fire being caused all over her entire butt was also serving to purge her guilt with him and the vigor that he was showing in administering the punishment was also a message that he was doing it out of love and not hate. SMACK!!! SMACK!!!SMACK!!!SMACK!!! SMACK!!! SMACK!!! SMACK!!! SMACK!!! SMACK!!!

As Peter's hand landed rapid whack after whack he held her struggling body close to him and watched her bottom go from dark pink to red to crimson.. He realized as he was doing it that there was still a bond there, and had always been with him. SMACK SMACK SMACK SMACK SMACK   All the regrets and frustrations of the past seven years were now landing on that upturned bottom squirming across his lap. SMACK!!! SMACK!!! SMACK!!! SMACK!!!!!! Finally she was bawling like a child now.

Suddenly, she realized that the sound of hand striking flesh was no longer dominating the room, but instead all she heard was herself crying and then softly weeping and then sniffling. Just when she was aware of that change, she felt him gently ease her off his lap and then he stood up himself. "I'm sorry I had to do that, Alicia, but I just had to." Before she could respond, he pulled her into his arms and hugged her and she quickly responded but throwing her arms around him and hugging him tight as well as she sobbed.

Then Alicia, with her teary eyes looked up to Peter's face. "I'm sorry, so sorry, too does that mean you really forgive me now?"

He gently wiped the tears from her cheeks and nodded. "I'm pretty sure these aren't the only tears you've shed the last seven years is it?"

She sniffled. "Actually they are, Peter. The first thing you learn in there, no crying, no weakness, you keep it all in."

"So that's why you asked me to do more?"

"I needed a good cry for me and to cry for you, too."

Peter placed her hand on the back of Alicia's neck and drew her to him and he kissed her and instantly Alicia responded as their tongues swirled together. When it was ended, Peter said: "There's something else you need ,too, isn't there?"

Alicia leaned her body closer to his. "I need to be a woman again." He leaned closer and brought her lips close to his as she continued. "More importantly I need to be a woman with the only man I really ever loved."

Peter's right hand went from her chin to the back of her neck and drew her mouth the last few inches to his and gave her a gentle brief kiss. Before he could pull back, Alicia placed her hand in back of his head and then began kissing and this time it seemed to go on forever.

Memories of so many other kisses they shared together flooded Alicia's mind now. Except for her stinging bottom, it was like the last seven years had been just a nightmare and they were together again. When the kiss ended, Alicia was almost panting and she knew that she was already wet and also could feel Peter's firmness against her. Alicia whispered: "Your kisses still get the juices flowing like no other man ever did."

He smiled through the tears. "So now it's my task to satisfy a horny woman"

She laughed just like that first time Peter had seen her. "Correction, very horny and you'll see how horny if you let me."

He smiled. "So is that a challenge?"

"You bet your ass it is, Sweetie." As she said this she gingerly pulled her panties back up and pulled her skirt back down.

He chuckled. "I'm not the one with a sore one."

She smiled. "But mine is the one that deserves to be."

Peter took his glass and motioned for her to do the same and then with his free hand took her hand. "If I am to do this, we're in the wrong room."

It was like Alicia was floating as Peter led her from Alan's old room into what had been their master bedroom. As she saw the room come into view it was almost the same as she left it the night she was arrested. "Damn!! It looks the same!" As she said it she nuzzled against him and was savoring the warmth of his body against her.

"I couldn't bear to change it."

Alicia understood and in that instant knew that for all his words and anger he had always loved her as well. They were getting closer to the bed. "I know why, Peter and that's I want this night to be so very special for the both of us. The only thing that would make it better is if I could hear our song again."

He smiled. You mean Peter Frampton's live version of *"Baby I Love Your Way?"*

"Oh you do remember, Sweetie!"

He walked over to his Ipod. "I still have it on here somewhere." He looked at it briefly. "Yes, here it is." He clicked on it and suddenly she heard the cheering crowd and then he started singing the slow melody. As it started, she walked to him and took him in her arms. "It's what we danced to at our wedding." He put his arms around her and they danced again to the song and she closed her eyes and could remember that magical night all over again.

83

When the song was over and she was in his arms, he whispered to her: "I love that outfit but I think it's outlived its usefulness tonight."

Alicia grinned. "It sure wasn't very useful when you had me across your lap."

He led her next to the bed. "This time you'll feel a lot when I get it off, baby" he said as he carefully removed her jacket and as he did she kicked off her shoes and noticed that Peter did the same with his loafers.

Alicia in turn started to loosen the buttons on Peter's shirt that allowed her to run her hands over his bare chest. "Mmmm still working out I see."

He chuckled. "Yeah it's been a form of escape for me."

"Probably not a good word to use around someone in my situation." They both laughed as he began unbuttoning her blouse as she had finished with the buttons on his shirt and was now working on loosening his belt. Once her blouse was unbuttoned he began to slip it off her as she moved her arms to assist him, and then in turn she did the same with his shirt so that Alicia only had the bra on above the waist and Peter was topless. Alicia part whispered and moaned: "Oh I always loved it when you stripped me down nice and slow."

He reached behind her and began to slowly unzip the back of her skirt. "Didn't I always tell you that the best presents are best unwrapped slowly?" As he said that, the skirt was loosened and fell to the floor and Alicia stepped out of them to reveal the pink lace panties.

Alicia by then had loosened Peter's belt and loosened his slacks and began to nudge them down his legs to reveal his dark blue boxer briefs."Mmmmm. I always loved hearing that. You have such a sexy voice and I still remember what is under those." She said as she laughed and patted his crotch.

"You know that laugh is what first made me notice you."

She wiggled around as Peter's hands cupped the bottom of her panties. "You never told me that!" As she said that, she leaned up to kiss him again and he returned it eagerly.

When the kiss was finished he reached around to unclasp her bra and then let it drop to the floor. Alicia felt like a teenager again when she knew that Peter was now able to gaze upon her breasts again. He reached out and gently squeezed her right breast, and she closed her eyes and let out a moan. "Oh you don't know how many nights I spent yearning to feel that again."

"Just focus on feeling it now, baby."

Her hand was now caressing Peter's briefs and she could tell it was tenting so very fast. "Feels like someone is getting himself ready." The seven year wait made part of her so eager to speed up and make love, but the wiser part realized that these moments needed to be one to be savored, and sipped like the last drops of that wine that was still in her glass. Peter had by now stepped out of his slacks and Alicia slipped her fingers under the waistband of the his briefs. "Speaking of presents time to unwrap this one after waiting for it for seven long years." She slowly lowered them down Peter's firm thighs and as she did her entire body shivered at the sight of a still gorgeous well defined penis popping out and aiming right at her. Oh how she remembered it so well and it was the one thing she always was dreaming during those lonely nights of feeling inside her again.

Right after he lowered her panties, he led her to the bed and draped her upon it but before he could do anything with her, she pulled him down on the bed as well and before he could react, flipped him on his back and turned her body to face his feet got on her hands and knees and then took his now even harder cock and placed her mouth over it. Over the years, she and Kristen had gotten very skilled orally and so began swirling her tongue around as she took it all in like she used to do with him years ago and started going up and down and the only noise on the room was a loud slurping sound.

"AHHHHHHHH!!" Peter began to thrust his hips.."Oh Gawd!!!" She thrust faster, but not too fast and there was a slight salty taste in her mouth now. "MMMMM Where did you learn that?"

She pulled off him now and his cock was pulsing and

glistening with her saliva and smiled. "Well some things I did learn over seven years, but it's a lot more fun with a man." As she said that, she was wiggling her butt and hips in front of his face.

"Hmmm, hinting at a 69?"

She chuckled. "More than hinting, Sweetie. Yup funny we never did that, but Kristen and me did often."

He grinned. "Well you don't have to be a genius to know how that works." He leaned forward and started licking her wiggling pussy and heard her moan even as she was going up and down Peter's seven and a half inches and as his tongue started eating her, she started going back and forth. Oh how she felt she was floating, even while she was observing that as far as technique was concerned, Kristen was better at it, and if she had been free time she'd teach Peter to do it better in the future. As Alicia instinctively spread her legs wider, Peter's tongue dove deeper into her. He stopped for a second and said: "Tonight I want to make that pussy of yours forget all about the last seven years."

"Mmmmmm" Alicia responded and as she continued to feast on Peter's manhood but always making sure she wasn't going so fast to make him explode. "Mmmmmm."

His tongue was darting in and out and back and forth and it only made her spread her legs even wider. She wanted him and craved to open as wide as she ever had to feel the warmth and the tickling way he moved around. He paused to look up. "Oh...damn I missed that very special way you taste. I could do this for hours and hours." Before she could react he dove back in and this time his tongue was moving up and down and around.

"AH AH AH AH AH" she panted as her hips were gyrating and having a life of her own as she pulled off him. "Ohhh Gawd" Then there was the scream the loud scream that let Peter know he had rediscovered that sweet spot.

He stopped again and as she was panting and then he firmly nudged her body off of him and onto her back while her legs remained splayed and bent at the knees. He looked down at her whiles he was still panting. "That's it, I want you to cum and cum so much that you are driven crazy." He dove back in and his tongue seemed possessed now and she was now panting and screaming loudly.

When he stopped and pulled his head up she was still panting. "Oh damn you got better."

"Remember it's your night. Got something else that I kept." He got up off the bed and went to the bottom drawer of what used to be her dresser and pulled out something and took it to a wall socket and plugged it in.

Alicia's eyes got wide. "You're going to use that, too?"

"Oh yes, dear. I still remember that the best way to get you warmed up was a good session with the vibrating wand."

Alicia was now squirming around because she remembered that only too well. "Mmmm you already have me hot."

"Hot? I want you flaming lava flowing hot, baby." He turned it on and the humming sound filled the room. "Let's see if I remember right." He brought it closer and closer to those pink lips between her legs and then touched then for a second and Alicia jumped. "Aha! Seems I do." He touched it again a little longer and she squirmed. "Yup now I remember."

"Mmmm you sure do, Sweetie." Now the wand went up and down. "Ohhh...ohhhh ahh....ah.....ah....ohhhhhhhhhhhhhhhhhhhhhhhhhh!"

"I want to see that pussy drip and pulse and hear you beg and beg." He kept it on and was going round and round with it as he now lifted her legs high in the air even as they were spread.

"Peter...please...ohhhh gawd....ohhhhh." However, as she said that, her hips were moving in unison with the wand.

"Had enough baby?"

"Oh gawd!!!! more...more....oh damn I love it!"

"Yeah that's my baby, but I won't let you cum just yet." He teased her just as she was close he'd pull it away.

"No please more, more!!!"

"In good time." He picked up the wand and this time ran it along the opening of her other hole that was so exposed.

"OHHHHHH damn!!!!!!" She wiggled around.

"Thought you might like that, I've been doing some research."

"MMMMM oh Peter Sweetie...ohhhhhh!!!" The wand went up and down as he held her legs with his free hand.

"That's right I'm going to get every inch of you aroused, baby." As the wand relentlessly wandered around that spot Alicia's legs struggled to escape and Peter suddenly released them and Alicia lowered her legs onto the bed, but they were still spread. "Now where were we before I got distracted? Oh yes that." The wand found her wet pussy again. Alicia's hips jerked off the bed before they slammed back down. "That's right I own that tonight, all of it."

"Mmmmm ohhhhh ohhhhh ah ah ah ah ah ah" Her panting echoed throughout the room now.

"Yes that's it I'm going to make you cum like an avalanche because now I've forgiven you."

"Forgiven me...mmmmm....mmmmm OHHHHHHHHHHHHHHHHHH! OHHHHHHHHHHHHHHHHH" Her hips were writhing and slithering around as her pussy tracked the path of the vibrator hungrily as his words seemed to trigger another intense orgasm.

"Yes baby, feel this because it's telling you that someone in the world still cares about you."

"OH gawwdddd!!!!
AWWWHHHHHWWWWWHHHHHHHHHHHH!" Her screams
filled the entire room "I'm cumming cumming again!! YES YES
YES!!!!" Her body was rocking back and forth and going up and
down wildly as the wand was being vigorously applied to her
throbbing clit.

"That's it baby, that's all I want to exist for you right now
is that wand and your pussy."

"Oh yes, YES" she screamed as another even more intense
orgasm overcame her. Even her most wonderful dreams over
these last years equaled this and she wasn't even feeling his
precious cock yet.

Finally he stopped and turned the wand off and leaned
over and kissed her and her tongue was telling him that she still
hungered to feel him inside her. Instead he went over to the
dresser and picked up the wine glasses and brought them over to
the bed and handed Alicia's glass to her. "I do remember you said
you wanted to talk over a glass of wine."

She laughed. "Peter Lowry, are you trying to tease me?"

He sat down next to her on the bed and put his free arm
around her shoulder and pulled her to him. "Maybe, but I also
think we can also talk while we cuddle a little." He kissed her
forehead. "Remember what I said, a present should be unwrapped
nice and slowly. I always want you to remember tonight."

"I will, Peter, thank you so very much." She leaned over and kissed him hard and deep.

Peter shuddered, because all that he had been thinking these last seven years was now in disarray. So far this night, she had been the same woman he had shared a bed with for over three years of marriage and knew that he'd never love another the way he loved her, and yet after tonight she would be gone again. Something gnawed at him and he had to know, even if it was painful.

"Why did you have to kill him, Alicia, why?"

He saw the tears again in her eyes and regretted asking, but he just had to know. "I don't know, I was unhappy with life and he was just so...so..."

"Abusive?"

She looked at him for a moment and paused. "I can't say that about him Peter. It was tempting to blame him, say it was his fault, and I thought of doing that seven years ago, but the lawyer said there wasn't evidence so it wouldn't work at a trial."

"But he was?"

She leaned over and kissed him on the forehead this time. "I wish it was actually abusive but it isn't. Jake could be a controlling jerk but I can see now that he didn't deserve to die. I was wrong and it was an evil thing to do."

"It was about the money then?"

"Well he's the one that insisted on the insurance and he bought some on my life, too but yes there was always the money but more like I wanted to escape. Life was so drab, he pestered me and always needed to know where I was every minute and saying I was never a good enough mother for the boys and he drove a truck long distance and frankly I realized that I was happier when he was away. I guess I had married too young and now I wanted out."

"You could have divorced."

"Yeah and been left with nothing. That family of his...uhhh...they would have made sure of that."

"So you felt trapped." As they spoke Peter reached over and was caressing her body. Somehow her confessions didn't repel him, but instead made him respect her honesty.

"Yeah that was a good way to put it. Then I began to fantasize how to get him out of my life and be free, and it's like this idea of killing him popped into my head and at first it was just a fantasy that I played out in my head but I was thinking more and more about it..."

"And suddenly you realized it might work?"

She nodded. "I dunno I was all nervous and all but kept saying it was just a thought but then it was a plan and then if you're gonna plan..."

Peter finished the sentence. "You should follow through"

She sniffled. "Yeah, so I decided to try an experiment. I knew one night he was off and so I just put some in his food to see if it made him drowsy...."

"And it worked?"

"Well I wasn't sure because it was so soon after that he got a call they needed someone to fill in. I panicked, I wasn't ready and still wanted the chance to back out. I begged him not to go and even stood at the door to block him but he said they'd pay time and a half so he shoved me away and his last words to me were "'Don't you ever tell me what to do, you dumb bitch!'" and then he left and then later I found out it happened."

"The accident?"

"Yeah, his truck went into another lane but he was the only one killed."

"And you couldn't tell him about the food?"

"How could I?"

"So you didn't intend it to happen then? Do you think you ever would have really done it?"

She sobbed. "I don't know. I've stared at the ceiling some nights and wondered if I would have and what things would have been like if he hadn't gotten that call. I don't know if I really had the nerve but the thing is that it happened, Peter."

"Did your lawyer know this?"

"Yeah he and my Mum knew but he said they'd never

believe it and even if I did by not telling him I was still guilty."

The realization that she was not that evil monster he thought she had been hit him. "Oh my God Alicia, oh my God." He rubbed his arm up and down her upper arm and shoulder, as his tone and heart softened even more. "Then later you met me."

She looked at him. "Yes, and somehow knew from that first night I saw you that you were my soulmate and I loved you and loved our life and I knew I'd done this terrible thing but hoped, just hoped that God would just spare me from suffering because of that mistake so I could make his sons and you happy. It was so wonderful and for those three years it was like being in heaven and then..."

"They found out."

"Yeah they couldn't accept what happened and then when it all fell apart I was wishing I could die right then and when I saw you looking at that dresser drawer I knew it was all over." She began to sob.

"I really was hoping they were wrong, that's why I looked."

"Like I said you didn't do anything wrong, Peter. Well that's the entire dirty story. You must hate me again, don't you?"

"No, baby I don't. You made a terrible mistake but I understand better now, and I know it wasn't done by the woman I married and grew to love." He leaned over and kissed her hard and she returned it with all her yearning.

"Does that mean we're still going to make love?"

"Wild horses couldn't stop me, baby."

As those words left his lips, Alicia got up and pounced to lay on top of him. "Well buster, after making this butt sore I'm sure not gonna lay on it right away!"

She was mounted on him and smiling as she looked down at his face. She moaned as he reached up with both hands and his fingers gently pressed each of her giggling but firm breasts. She looked down and saw his throbbing tool sticking straight up and took it eagerly in her hands and heard a sensual low moan come from his lips. "That's right, Sweetie, I'm gonna give it a good slow deep ride." He moaned even more as she lifted up enough to guide his manhood towards her hot wet pussy. "That's right, it's time for it to come back home again."

It was the moment she had been dreaming of for seven years as she steadied his cock and slowly impaled herself upon it. This was the moment she had often thought of as the sensation of her being able to take a man was occurring once again. She knew it was a stolen moment, and one the law had never intended to happen and yet miraculously here it was. "MMMMM MMMMM" Peter moaned as his hips slightly thrust upward to meet her.

"That's right it's become so very hungry and is going to

devour every inch of you over and over again!"

"Ow gawd Alicia, it's as good as I remembered!" She pulled back up and then thrust back down slowly and closing her eyes and relishing that feeling once again to feel that hard gorgeous rod inside her. Oh how she had missed it and had craved to experience it once again. She shivered as she was aware of it throbbing inside her as she made it slowly slide up and down inside her. She craved and pushed to feel every single inch of him. She wanted him so much but she deliberately teased him by going at a leisurely pace because she wanted to burn into her mind the memory of this sensation that would need to last the rest of her life. "Ohhhh faster, faster" Peter moaned.

"You're not the only one who knows how to tease."

Peter placed his mouth over Alicia's right nipple and began to lick and suck it, and Alicia let out a long groan and began to thrust faster and as she did he moved to the left nipple then back to the right and soon he was going back and forth between the two rapidly. It had the desired effect as Alicia was now thrusting harder and faster but then as she held her hips up, Peter took up the slack and was pumping up his hips rapidly as his shaft became a piston pumping into the awaiting steamy and sopping cavern.

The room was filled with the moans and groans of two lovers rediscovering a love that had once been lost to them as they became as one and were writhing and screaming in unison as their long denied ecstasy was fulfilled at last. Alicia slowed down but pushed all the way down to make sure that she felt every quiver of his orgasm inside her, and then she collapsed on top of him. When she did, she placed her arms around him and rested her head against his and looked dreamily at him.

They were both still panting as he opened his eyes and looked upon her while his hand began caressing and playing with her hair. "You never were that assertive before either" he said grinning.

"So after seven years hanging out with such fine people as I do I'm not the same innocent girl that I was before?"

"You thought you were innocent, huh? I always described you as exciting and you're even more so now."

"Next time it'll be your turn to take charge."

"Believe me I will because this wasn't the end of it."

"Mmmmmmm." Alicia replied as he pulled her mouth to his and they exchanged a kiss. After kissing they just lay there together silently and felt each other breathing and feeling the warmth flowing from each other's body. "I feel like it's a dream and I'm so afraid I'm going to wake up and realize it wasn't real."

He put placed a finger to her lips. "Sh., Sh." Then he used the same hand to caress her right cheek. "It is real, and it will always be real for both of us and nobody can ever take it away from us no matter what they do."

"Oh Peter I love you so much and always have."

"I know that now, even if I forgot it once."

"Just being able to be here with you, and feeling you next to me makes me feel so complete."

"We still have the rest of the night, baby."

"But then....."Alicia responded as she started to sob.

Once again Peter's finger touched her lips."Sh. Don't ruin what we have tonight there, As you said it's a gift, a miraculous gift."

"Not so miraculous, Peter. There will be a price to pay when I get back there."

Peter's eyes teared up. I know it means you have to go back to that place after your Mum's funeral."

She shifted her body so she was laying on her side next to him. "If it was just that I might be able to deal with it. Kristen and me got on alright..."

"Who's Kristen?"

"My cellmate."

"Did you become lovers?"

"As much as you can be in prison. We're nice to each other and she's taught me a lot and kept me out of trouble but it's gonna be different when I get back."

Peter was puzzled. "How different?"

99

"Well Alex...I mean Ms. Foreman made me agree that when I get back there she'll...she'll." She started to cry.

"She'll what, baby?"

"Have her way with me one day a week."

"What are you talking about, Alicia?"

"You know what have her way means Peter."

"How is that possible, Alicia?"

"I don't know but I had to sign something to let them do it. I'm scared."

"Why did you sign it then?"

"If I didn't I'd never be let out here and I'd never see you again!"

"I'm sorry, I just don't know what to do, I mean if higher ups knew wouldn't they do something?"

"They might but when they did they'd make my life a living hell. Nobody likes a snitch."

He rolled over on top of her and was able to admire her body. She had such beautifully toned legs that rose to those gorgeously round butt cheeks that were still pink from his chastisement and he couldn't resist the temptation to begin massaging her.

"Mmmmm, Sweetie," she said as his strong but sensual hands began to kneed her flesh that craved to feel him so much. The warmth and firmness of her body only served to make him hunger even more to penetrate her and as she squirmed and moaned he leaned down and planted a gentle kiss on the back of her neck and as his hands resumed their journey over her entire body. His greatest desire now was to explore every single inch of her and wanted her to feel his hand touching her to show his true feelings for her.

"You are so sexy, baby." Even on her stomach she could feel his hardness and knew she was also wet again. "Right now I want you to feel like you are floating on a cloud." He leaned and turned her face to his and kissed her deeply and long.

She wiggled around and was able to turn over to face him and he began to massage her shoulders, breasts and stomach,before his hands traced a path down her legs and slightly squeezed her thighs and legs. As he did,his hand grazed that wet spot between her legs as he teased it lovingly. "Oh Peter it's like I'm in a dream."

"It's real, baby." As he said that, he guided his manhood to that special place and guided it in and as he did he moved up and down and made her moan again. "This time I'm gonna ride you hard and long and make you forget all about that other stuff, understand?"

She looked up and grinned. "Wouldn't have it any other way" but then he pulled up and pushed down.....Uh...Uh"

Peter closed his eyes, and even as his rod was basking in

the moist, hot and ravenous flesh that he allowed to finally possess it, he was also thinking of what Alicia had just told him. It meant this had to the best he could ever give her, he was determined to pound and pound her and let her know that in his mind she would always be his even if they would be apart after tonight. "I always want you to remember this moment, baby."

Even as his pleasure was reaching a fever pitch, he found himself beginning to cry at the loss that he knew was coming, and trying to fathom how she would ever have the strength to endure it even as he was sucking hard on each of her breasts in turn or alternating by kissing her. As he felt her squirming and mutual thrusts, and the sweat and heat of her body it was as if they were just a single being again and he could almost feel himself merging totally with her mind and feeling her delight as she experienced his orgasm and explosion as it occurred instantaneously with hers did and it made them soar together above everything before they finally came back down gently to earth and he his body dropped softly back down on top of her as they were both panting again.

Peter was breathing hard as he looked down upon Alicia's face that looked so serene. "This was even better than it was before."

Alicia's eyes opened and her fingers began to trace lazy lines on his chest as she played with it. "It'll get better next time, Sweetie." She sobbed again as her own words seem to hit her.

"Next time. Soon there won't be a next time because I have to go back there to grow old and ugly and never see you again!" She looked away and sobbed even more. "I'm only thirty four, and you see, I'm still young, and have so much to give you. Why did Jake have to be so hard-headed and not listen to me when I tried to stop him!" Then she sobbed even more. "I can't bear to leave you Peter, I wish I could die instead."

Peter held her and rocked her body as she continued to sob because at that moment he knew what he had to do. "I hope you know I'd do anything, anything to spare you from that heartache, baby."

Alicia smiled at him through her glistening eyes. "Would you really? Do you love me that much?"

"Maybe I didn't understand things before but now I do. I'll always love you, baby, always." As he said that he picked up the wand. "And I still have more time for me to show you."

Humming, and moaning and screams of delight now filled the room as Peter was determined for Alicia's to enjoy every pleasure he could give her while there was still time. He watched and felt her body contort as orgasm after orgasm overwhelmed her.

As he put the wand down and saw her still heaving, she looked up at him. "I really, really need to have you, not just that wand one more time. One last time."

He looked at the clock in the room and saw that it said seven forty five and it was already light outside. "Then that's what you're going to have, baby." As he began to understand even more what he needed to for her, he said: "First let me get us each another glass of Chardonnay."

She smiled. "Mmmm how decadent, wine in the morning. Yes it would be nice to have a last glass of that, too."

He leaned down and kissed her. "After we drink it together, I'm going to make this very, very special, baby."

Her eyes teared up. "Yes, one last very special time. I need that, Sweetie."

Peter pulled on his briefs and slippers and plodded down the stairs with the two almost empty glasses. He went into the kitchen and carefully rinsed both glasses and carefully wiped them thoroughly off with a cloth. Still holding the cloth, he held each glass with the cloth and placed them on the counter and glanced over at the canister where he knew something was stored and after one important but small step, he poured the wine into each glass, and then wiped the bottle off with the cloth as well. Holding her glass with a small cloth he gingerly climbed the stairs to make sure he didn't spill any of the precious fluid and saw her laying on the bed with her eyes closed but then they opened and he saw her smile.

He was careful to hand her the glass on the left and kept

the other for himself and then discreetly dropped the cloth to the floor. He held his glass in the pose of a toast "Here's to being with the one you love, Alicia."

She grinned. "Yes, the only one I love, Peter."

He remembered the time when they were married when during the holidays he took her to see "*The Nutcracker*" and there was the scene when the main characters danced to "*Pas de Deux*" when they knew it was time for them to part because the dream was over, and that song and scene was playing over and over in his mind now.

Peter's eyes filled with tears again while the tune kept going in his head as he stripped off his briefs again. "Drink up so I can show you even more how much I love you." He watched her drink from her glass as he did the same. After she drank almost all of it she placed her glass onto the night table as he did the same with his. "I want this to be tender and perfect, Alicia." As he said that he decided to play "*Pas de Deux*" on his Ipod as well as they made love.

She eagerly took his manhood in her mouth and then after a few minutes leaned back as Peter mounted her. "Oh that is so sad, but was also very romantic. Make this one slow and loving like the song, Peter."

His eyes glistened as he responded. "Yes because I want to make it last for eternity."

105

He eased himself into her and the warmth and tightness immediately made him throb. "MMMM eternity, that sounds so wonderful I really do wish it could last that long."

He gently massaged each of her breasts. "If you close your eyes, baby and take it all in,maybe it will,baby."

"Oh Peter...ohhh....ohhh...you were always so good...mmmmmmm" Her legs were now wrapped around him and he could feel her muscles tightening and holding him tight to her.

"That's it baby, that's how much I love you." He was thrusting faster and feeling her begin to writhe under him. The heat of her body was mingling with his and the sweat began to form between them.

"Oh gawd I never wanted to lose you..."

"You haven't because you will always be in my heart, baby." He was doing all he could to fight back the tears.

Just then her back arched and her legs pressed around him even harder "MMMMM MMMMM oh gawd......" In that same moment, he felt himself getting rock hard and then exploding once again inside her and they were both emitting moans and screams of pleasure and release.

Then as they began to relax together while he was still inside her he felt a different kind of shudder from her as she looked up at him, and he leaned down. "Uh..uh I feel strange....Peter?"

He was now lightly caressing her breasts and her face. "It's OK, Alicia just relax, it's probably just the wine."

"Just the wine?"

"Yes baby, just close your eyes and everything will be fine."

Her voice was getting sleepy as her eyes began to droop. "MMMM yes. I feel so sleepy. Oh I love being with you."

"You always will be, baby and this will also make sure you'll always be young and beautiful, free and loved. Just close your eyes and let it happen."

"Oh, I'm so tired, Sweetie. All I ever wanted is to be loved by you."

Peter leaned down and by now was crying as he kissed her. "You have that Alicia and you always will and now you'll never have to go back to that awful place."

Her eyes fluttered slightly. "Oh Peter, I'd give anything..."

His voice quivered "Yes baby, I know. Anything not to be locked up, or knowing you'd just grow old and die alone in prison and be apart from the one you love."

Her voice was so very soft now and he thought he could actually see her smile. "Oh Sweetie I won't have to anymore,will I?"

"No baby, I've made sure of it."

"Oh thank you Peter, thank you."

"And after it happens I'll make sure you'll be wearing something beautiful, too."

"MMMM something beautiful like the red dress I wore to meet you..... I feel so cold Peter, please hold me."

He sobbed as took her head in his arms and gently rocked her. "I'll always hold you baby."

Her voice was distant and barely audible. "I love you so, please kiss me."

He leaned down and his lips met hers and they kissed briefly before her tongue stopped moving. He ended the kiss."Yes it's time for you to finally rest and find your peace with your Mum."

Peter wept and the tears flowed down his face because he knew that she was gone. He knew she had meant it when she had said she'd rather die then be forced to go back in there and so he had loved her enough to grant her wish. Looking down at her naked body he knew he had made a promise and would make sure she was wearing that would emphasize the beauty that she still had, even in death. He wanted them to gaze upon the woman that he had married, loved and then made love to, not the convict she had been the last seven years.

He knew there was one more song that would be fitting for the occasion. He went to his Ipod once again and played "*Nearer My God To Thee*" as he went into the closet and found a bright red dress just like the one she had been wearing when he had first met her, and that she had described in her last wish and slowly began to dress her. First the panties, the bra and then it took a lot of maneuvering to get the dress over her unresponsive and limp body and then he lined a pair of red dress shoes against the bed.

He lovingly straightened her out on the bed so that she was face up with her head resting on the pillow and when he was done he leaned down and planted a final kiss on her still lips. Her body that had been so hot with passion only minutes ago was already now cooling down just as the song ended and the room was silent.

Fighting back his tears, he lifted up Alicia's limp left hand and placed her fingers briefly around his wine glass to make sure her fingerprints were on both glasses as if she had carried both glasses upstairs instead of him and then carefully used the cloth to place it back on the night table to join hers and then left them there together. Then he got dressed and picked the cloth back up from the floor and brought it back down with him as he slowly walked down the stairs in the now silent and lonely house. After folding the cloth back and returning it to its place on the kitchen counter he took a deep breath as he looked out the window and saw the gray car parked outside.

He took a deep breath and then forcefully opened the front

door and ran out to the car in an agitated state and the car door quickly opened.

"Is anything wrong, Sir? It's not nine o'clock yet."

The tears were still flowing down Peter's face as he looked over at Liam and spoke to him in a quavering voice. "Please help me! I can't wake her up!" He continued to sob. "I think something is wrong with her, terribly wrong!"

xxxxxx

The End

H. Matt Synnot